RACE TO KILL

RACE TO KILL

A Love and Scandal Novel

RACHEL KALL

Race To Kill
Copyright © 2013 by Rachel Kall
Ebook ISBN: 9781625172754
ISBN-13: 9781492394051

NYLA Publishing
350 7th Avenue, Suite 2003, NY 10001, New York.
http://www.nyliterary.com

For Susan, for being the best friend that everyone should be lucky enough to have.

ACKNOWLEDGEMENTS

I am so grateful to those people who helped make this dream a reality. To my amazing agent, Sarah Younger, and the entire team at Nancy Yost Literary Agency. You inspire me, support me, and believe in me. I am so happy to have you on my side and traveling on this journey with me. To Aaron for always listening to my story ideas. To Susan for being the best cheerleader and friend a girl could ever ask for. To my five wonderful furkids who love me unconditionally. To my writer friends who not only encourage me to reach for the stars, but who are a source of joy and friendship. And last but not least, to my mom for always providing support, encouragement, and love.

CHAPTER ONE

Two Weeks Ago

Marc Locke cursed under his breath. And then he cursed again as he sat up in his uncomfortable office chair and watched his boss walk into the room. This operation was going to be more difficult than he first thought.

"Did you hear me, Locke?" The gruff voice of Peter Crown, his newly appointed boss at the FBI, interrupted his thoughts.

"Yes, sir. Sorry." Marc focused his attention back on Peter's serious dark eyes.

"We've found you a way into the Nelson presidential campaign." Peter took a seat across from him. "The evidence indicating illegal contributions is mounting against the Senator, but we need someone on the inside to put together all the pieces. I want to believe the Senator's innocent, but God only knows what his staff is up to. Under the new campaign contribution laws, things have gotten murky."

Marc knew the case inside and out. Peter sounded like he was trying to convince himself that he was making the right call. Marc leaned back in his chair and waited for Peter to tell him something he didn't know.

"So you're going in undercover as a security specialist. I know your file. Your military background makes you a perfect fit. Now that Nelson is his party's nominee for President, the Secret Service will be providing security. But the candidate always wants their own personal staff too, and you'll fill that role working at Nelson campaign headquarters. Uncovering political corruption is a high priority for the FBI. There can't be an ounce of partisanship or our investigation will be DOA." Peter leaned forward in his seat and flattened his hands across the large wooden desk. "We need credibility. Your record with us is impeccable. So don't screw up."

"I won't screw up," Marc said, believing each word. Because this time he wouldn't. He still had a lot to atone for.

Peter raised an eyebrow. "Good. Get the job done. That's all I ask. Follow the evidence wherever it leads you and report back. Understood?"

"Yes, sir."

Peter nodded and walked out of his office. Peter was a nice enough guy, but he was too much of a paper pusher for Marc's taste. At the FBI he got to put away bad guys for a living—and with a lot less stress on his body than being a member of Delta Force. Or at least that was the reason he gave anyone who asked him why he left the military.

The idea of being a security consultant was intriguing, or maybe he'd end up being just hired muscle. He'd have to see which way he wanted to play it. He was glad to be back in the field. The past six months at a desk left him itching for more, but what he had accomplished was impressive. Convincing the higher ups at the Bureau to open an official investigation into Senator Nelson's campaign financing was huge. He was driven to uncover the truth. The thought of all his friends, his brothers in arms, who lost their lives fighting for the country made his temper flare. Why should they fight for a country that was full of crooked politicians?

He didn't have anything against Senator Nelson specifically, but he hated politicians who had corrupt campaign finance systems. There was so much money in politics through legal means. Why did the pols now have to start illegal campaign financing too? Given the sensitive nature of the campaign, Peter was right. The last thing he wanted was to be seen as one of President Helen Riley's operatives. The FBI wanted the truth and so did he. It was time to go get hired for the job.

* * *

Present Day

The doctor didn't know if Gene would make it. The harsh words replayed over and over again in Viv's head. As she sat alone in the waiting room, she needed to gather herself before she went to Senator Nelson's campaign headquarters. A hot tear slid town her cheek. Gene was a true mentor to her—a father figure. And now because of this heart attack, he might die. Another person she cared about gone forever. Death seemed so real to her at the moment. A heavy burden weighed on her heart. What was she going to do if Gene didn't make it? What was the Nelson campaign going to do? Gene was the backbone of the campaign. As the lead campaign spokesman, he was not only the face, but a good part of the brains behind Senator Nelson's bid for the presidency.

Maybe the hard-fought primary had taken its toll. Gene worked around the clock, but he had for years. Viv couldn't believe it had finally caught up to him. Was a political campaign worth paying the ultimate price? She shook her head knowing that Gene would answer that question a fervent yes. He believed in what Senator Nelson stood for and had been fighting his entire life for the party.

Her phone buzzed, and she read the text message. It was from Arthur Rubio, Nelson's chief campaign strategist. Otherwise known as her nemesis. He wanted to see her right away. Could things get any worse? She and Arthur didn't see eye to eye. Ever. But he was next in charge after Gene, so now she basically reported to him. Who knows what he wanted?

By the time she reached campaign headquarters, her pulse raced. When she opened the door, she was met by a flurry of activity. Everyone was on high alert. Not only was Gene incapacitated, the latest tracking polls showed a five point lead for the President. A group of young student volunteers were answering the phones, and a flood of voices filled the main room. She waved to a few of the volunteers and made her way back to the private area for higher ranking staff.

Of course, higher ranking was relative. She was the most junior person of the group, but she didn't back down. After working under Gene for a year, she had learned more than most people could in a lifetime. And it wasn't like she was a kid fresh out of college.

Her three-inch heels were not her friend today, but since she was so short she had to wear them to put her closer to eye level with her peers. She checked to make sure she looked presentable, smoothed down her suit jacket, and knocked lightly before she entered the office. Senator Jeff Nelson sat surrounded by his two top campaign staff members.

"Vivian," the Senator said. "Glad you could join us."

"Sorry I'm late, sir. I was at the hospital."

"Any more word on Gene?" The Senator's eyes darkened.

"No." She caught her breath. "He's still in critical condition. And…" She looked down and felt like she couldn't say what the doctor had reported. There was a chance Gene wouldn't make it. She forced herself to say something else. "It's touch and go, Senator."

"He's got the best heart doctor around working on him. Gene's a tough son of a bitch. He's going to pull through, Viv."

She nodded and took a seat. The Senator was flanked by Arthur on one side and Abby Morris, the chief political director, on the other.

The Senator stood up from his chair and took a big gulp of his coffee. He commanded the room. A tall and slender man, his short gray hair perfectly styled. But his face showed the toll of the campaign. She hoped that he wouldn't have a heart attack too. At fifty five, he was still relatively young and in great shape, but she couldn't help but worry.

"We've got a huge void here, people," the Senator said.

Arthur rolled up his sleeves. "I've already put out feelers. We should have a replacement for Gene within a few days. And in the meantime, Governor Banks will be stepping up his media spots. That's what Vice Presidential candidates do. Fill the void. When we picked him as your VP choice we knew he was versatile."

"Actually, Arthur," the Senator said. "I want the Governor to stay on the campaign trail. He's by far our best campaigner and has real traction in key swing states. I have something else in mind."

"Like what, sir? We need to get Gene's replacement ASAP. I don't need to tell you about our drop in the polls. We were running even. This race is tight."

"I couldn't agree more. Which is why Vivian should be my new campaign spokesperson."

Viv almost fell out of her chair. She had to be delusional from lack of sleep. There was no way she'd just heard the Senator say that.

"Senator, with all due respect," Arthur said. "Viv was the number two under Gene, but she's what, thirty years old?"

All eyes in the room turned to her. "I'm actually thirty two."

Arthur stood up and started pacing.

"Wait, wait," Abby chimed in. "Don't dismiss this, Arthur."

"Has everyone lost their minds, here?" Arthur no longer tried to hide his surprise at Nelson's suggestion.

"No, Arthur, wait. You're the one not thinking strategically," Abby said. "President Riley has a lock on the female vote right now. We need to do something to shake up that demographic. Who better to criticize the first woman president than another woman? A young, attractive, and highly educated woman. How many degrees do you have again, Viv?"

Before Viv could answer, Arthur cut in. "I don't care if she graduated first in her class from Harvard. This is a presidential campaign, not an intellectual exercise. And we went from dead even to a five point drop in the polls in the past week."

"All the more reason to make a big move against Helen while we can," Abby scoffed. She pushed her curly auburn hair behind her ear. "Arthur, you've been running this campaign your usual way. It's worked before, but the times are changing now. Why not let us try something different? We'll monitor the polls. Just give me some time with Viv. If we aren't seeing results, we can go to someone else. How does that sound, Senator?"

"Sounds like a plan to me. And I know well enough about Viv's schooling. She interned for me when she was at Georgetown."

Arthur opened his mouth, and the Senator lifted his hand to silence him. "I'd like to talk to Viv for a moment in private."

Arthur crossed his arms and huffed as he left the room along with Abby. Viv's hands felt sweaty, and she wondered if Arthur was right. Was she ready for this?

The Senator took a seat beside her. "I wanted to talk to you about this alone before I brought it to the group, but things were escalating quickly. I needed to go ahead and make a decision."

Was he really apologizing to her? "Sir, I don't know what to say. What if Arthur's right? Being your spokesperson is a huge responsibility." Could she really do this?

"Vivian Reese, you're one of the smartest people on my staff. Yeah, you're young, but you're hungry. You know your stuff. I won't be worried about you being in over your head on the substance. And you'll get used to being in front of the national camera soon enough."

"Sir, you know I'll do my best. I believe in what we're doing here. I think the President's going down the wrong path on so many issues I care deeply about."

He reached over and patted her shoulder. "Your enthusiasm shines through. Voters will see it. I have no doubts this is the right move." He hung his head low. "I'm sick about Gene, but he wouldn't want us to cave now. There's too much at stake."

"I know that's true. Gene would want us fighting. Especially with the slight lead the President's taken in the polls."

"Listen to Arthur." He stood. "But don't let him get inside your head. You are exactly the type of voter I need to win this election."

Abby poked her head back into the room. "I'm sorry, Senator, but we need to leave to make your next appointment."

"We're done here." He nodded in Viv's direction.

The Senator walked out of the room, and Viv took a moment to herself. What had just happened? One minute she was an assistant spokesperson for the campaign. Now she was *the* spokesperson for Senator Nelson's presidential campaign. Yeah, she did appearances, but Gene had handled all of the national coverage. He was a pro, and she couldn't perform at his seasoned level. The Senator was right, though. All she could do was be herself. She hadn't worked all these years to give up now and have Arthur fill her spot with one of his friends. Couldn't she bring something fresh into the campaign? She sure hoped so. If she didn't, she'd soon be out of a job.

***

The next afternoon Viv stepped out of her car and smoothed down her black pantsuit and adjusted her purple blouse. *This isn't that big of a deal,* she told herself. This was a trial run. Yeah, it was a national TV spot, but it wasn't going to be a hostile interview.

They'd chosen her first foray on the national news as the new spokesperson wisely. Or Abby had. And she would be doing the show via satellite from campaign headquarters.

She walked up to the main entrance and swore, realizing she'd left her credentials and badge in the car. Oh well, someone there would know her. She'd spent a lot of her time lately in the Florida office. Florida was a key swing state in the election. But now with her unexpected promotion, she would be working out of the Washington, DC office. A perk of working for a Senator from Virginia. Arthur had made the strategic decision to set up shop there because he thought it made Nelson seem more presidential. And while she was glad to be living back home in her own condo, Viv questioned his position. She thought it made the Senator seem more inside the beltway than he already was. That's one reason she enjoyed working in the South Florida office of the campaign. She felt connected to people in the local community; real people, with real problems.

Viv walked through the door and ran into a human brick wall.

"Sorry, ma'am. I need to see your identification," a deep voice said.

Viv looked up—way up into the dark chocolate eyes of the huge man blocking her way. Good grief, he had a foot on her. At least. She hadn't worn her highest heels today because she knew she'd be sitting for the interview. Now she wished she had.

"I left my badge in my car," she said. She tapped her foot with impatient nerves.

"I'll need you to go get it." His face remained passive, and he didn't break eye contact.

"I'm going to be late." She looked down at her watch. "Crap, I'm going live in less than ten minutes. This is a national TV spot. I can't be late. Let me by." She took a step forward, and he blocked her path. Obviously she wasn't going to get past him if he didn't want her to.

He cocked his head to the side. "I haven't seen you around here before."

"And I haven't seen you either. I'm taking over for Gene."

"You're the new spokesman?" His eyes widened.

"Spokesperson," she corrected him.

"Excuse me." He smiled and shifted his weight. "Anyone around here who can vouch for you? How do I know you're not here to harass the Senator?"

"Give me a break." She was exasperated by his tactics, but she couldn't help but look closer at him. His arms bulged under his tailored navy dress shirt. His dark brown hair was cut short, and a hint of tiny stubble covered his jaw.

"God, where have you been?" Abby's voice rang in her ear.

"Sorry, I got detained by—I didn't get your name?" She motioned to the security hunk.

"Name is Marc. Marc Locke," he said, his eyes twinkling.

"Great, you've met the private security." Abby grabbed her arm. "We've got to get going."

Abby was pushing her into the media room where she'd do the interview. "Do you remember the talking points?"

"I drafted them, Abby."

"That's right." Abby shook her head and started pacing.

"Abby, I'll be fine. I promise."

"Sorry, not meaning to stress you out." She paused. "Thank God, Gene's going to pull through. But he definitely won't be back to the campaign."

Viv had heard the news last night that Gene was in stable condition. It was a huge weight lifted off her shoulders.

Abby fussed with Viv's suit jacket. "This is your time to shine, but I'm not going to sugarcoat it. If you don't perform, Arthur will pounce." Abby took a step back, surveying Viv. "You look great. Get in the hot seat. The tech guys have everything set up. And I know you wrote the talking points, but remember, push the Senator's record on women's issue. Let's hit them hard right out of the gate."

Viv nodded, but she had her own ideas. She didn't want to be seen as a token, which is exactly what would happen if she pushed women's issues too hard. This was live TV. She had to keep it together.

The lights blinked on and it was game time. It was like Viv wasn't even in her own body. The questions were pretty straight forward and nothing she couldn't handle. She felt herself smile, and she tried to not look tense. On the inside, though, every muscle and fiber in her body was on high alert. She couldn't screw this up. Not her big chance. The five minute TV spot flew by. Once the feed went dead, Viv took a deep breath. She had made it through her first national TV interview with no major mistakes. Even though Arthur wasn't in the office, she knew he'd be watching and ready to jump on any sign of weakness. She pushed her shoulders back and lifted up her chin. She wasn't going to let that happen. The door opened and Abby walked in.

"That was excellent, Viv." Abby put one hand on her hip and used the other to push up her glasses. "You didn't do as I asked on the women's issues front, but I think your approach worked. We'll have to see if there's any reaction with the voters."

"Thanks," Viv said.

"At any rate, you did more than enough to fend off Arthur for the time being."

Viv looked at Abby and decided to pry. "What's up with security stud?"

"Ah, that's our chief security consultant, Marcus Locke. We've got Secret Service coverage for the Senator, but everyone felt better also having private security helping here at headquarters.

Marc is in charge of that effort. It's a bit of an annoyance, but you'll get used to him. You won't even know he's around."

Yeah right, she thought. How could she not notice this Locke guy?

Abby walked over closer to her. "You've got a friend in the President's campaign, right?"

Viv averted her eyes. The last thing she wanted to do was to have the campaign get in the way of her friendship with Serena. "I do, but we keep our friendship separate for obvious reasons."

Abby nodded and sighed. "I know she's your friend, but if you happen to get anything from her, please pass it along. All's fair in love, war, and politics. Get some rest. Your next appearance is tomorrow. Can't have you looking too tired." Abby turned and took a step and then looked over her shoulder. "Again, great job."

Viv felt herself beaming. She couldn't hide her excitement in a job well done. She had been a student of politics and foreign affairs for a long time, and she finally felt like she was using her degrees. Inside she knew she was a nerd even though outside she didn't look like one. Maybe she'd invite Serena out of a drink tonight to celebrate her first national TV spot.

Viv walked out of the media room, and her eyes immediately met Marc's. He strode over to her. "Nice job. Everyone out here was watching.""Thanks. I guess we need to be formally introduced to each other. I'm Vivian Reese. Everyone calls me Viv."

He reached out his hand which was strong and warm when he took hers. "I'm Marcus Locke. People call me Marc or Locke." He winked and smiled mischievously.

So he was going to be a flirt. Viv wasn't all that surprised given his appearance. Women probably fell all over him on a regular basis. Looking up at him she almost had to strain her neck because of the height difference.

She took a step back. "I hear you're the head security guy here. I didn't see you yesterday."

"I'm here most of the time, but I was called out yesterday," he said.

"I've been mostly working out of the Florida office."

"Hablo Espanol?" he asked in perfect Spanish.

"No, not much. Just a little to get by. I'm better with European languages."

"Oh, really? Like what?" His eyes widened.

She was sure he probably thought she was just another pretty face. "I speak Russian fluently and a bit of French and German."

"I'm impressed. With your new job it looks like we'll be seeing a lot of each other then."

"You're just here as a precaution, right?"

"Yes, ma'am. It's pretty standard operating procedure to have private security at this stage in the campaign. We also have a limited Secret Service presence here at headquarters too."

She felt herself reacting to his smooth voice. The last thing she needed to think about was a hot fling with an even hotter security guard. But oh, couldn't a girl dream? Just for a minute. "I assume you're a supporter of the Senator."

He pursed his lips together. "I'm not that political. More of a good soldier type."

She knew it. He had military written all over him. Just like her Navy SEAL ex.

"Special Forces?" she asked.

"Delta Force." He laughed. "Am I that obvious?"

She walked a step toward him and looked him over. "Uh, yeah. You pretty much scream it. I've seen a lot of your type."

"My type?" he asked with an incredulous look. "Now, I don't like the sound of that…"

"It is what it is." Her hot little fantasy was shattered. She'd sworn after Scott had broken her heart that she'd stay away from alpha males. Why couldn't he just be a hunky security guard? That gleam in his eyes told her he was already strategizing. Another thing that bothered her. But she wouldn't be outmaneuvered. This guy had no idea who he was dealing with.

"Maybe we can grab a drink sometime and you can make a more educated determination about me?" He leaned up against the wall behind him and crossed his arms on his chest.

"Maybe." She could play this game for a bit, but she didn't trust Marc Locke. Not one bit.

* * *

Marc watched as Viv walked out the door, and he felt his temperature continue to rise. Yeah, she was hot. Not necessarily his type. A short fireball of a brunette. But did he even have a type as long as they only came home with him once? She had long dark hair that fell well past her shoulders. In contrast to her dark hair, she had striking blue eyes. The kind of eyes he fell for in bars late at night. One night was about all he could handle with most women—two max. Unfortunately, Viv might be caught up in his investigation. She looked harmless enough, but he knew better than to believe that. He thought her an odd choice to replace Gene. Maybe they wanted a female face to combat the President. Could be a smart political move.

She might be hot, but he needed to do his leg work on her. He'd already been vetting all of the other key staffers and building the relevant evidence for his investigation. But this Viv added a new wrinkle to things. Gene had been clean, he'd established that, but who knew about Viv? He learned a long time ago that looks could be deceiving. Hell, the woman spoke Russian. She wasn't just a TV face for the campaign. She had to be a lot more. And did she have the ear of the Senator? He'd find out. First he'd investigate her connections to the major donors. Had she really been spending her time in Florida? He had a full plate of questions, and he was ready for some answers.

He hated the political scene, but he loved his job at the FBI because he actually got to crack down on corruption for a living. No, it wasn't kicking ass in the middle of a God forsaken desert, but it still felt pretty good. It wasn't like *all* politicians were good for nothing, but in his experience most of them were. The fact that President Riley was a woman made no difference to him. It just meant she put a softer face on a reality that was all too harsh. He'd seen more in his years in the military than he'd ever need to see again to know life wasn't fair. American freedom didn't come without a price.

The lead Secret Service agent stationed on site walked over to him. Ralph Major was annoying. He was so cocky. Marc hadn't seen him in action, but figured he had to be good to be tasked to this high profile campaign.

"I saw you checking out Viv. You want a piece, huh?" Ralph punched him in the arm.

"Is that all you think about, Ralph?"

"Man, don't tell me you aren't thinking the exact same thing. You'd have to be an idiot not to."

"And you shouldn't even think about going there. Isn't that some Secret Service violation?"

Ralph laughed and smacked him on the back. "Believe it or not, I can be discreet. Just biding my time. So if you want a chance at her, I've given you fair warning there will be some healthy competition. But don't worry. You can have her when I'm done."

Okay, Marc wasn't the best at relationships, but he wasn't that much of a slime ball. "Nice talking to you, Ralph. As always." Marc looked down at his watch and saw his shift was over. He was more than ready to get out of campaign headquarters. And start his inquiry into Ms. Vivian Reese.

***

He'd seen her on TV now three times. It was almost like she was the perfect mix between an angel and a devil. So pure but tempting at the same time. Her porcelain skin and piercing blue eyes spoke to him. But why was she supporting that monster? Every word out of her mouth was a lie. Those beautiful pink lips filled with lies. What she needed was some direction from a man like him. Yeah, he had his orders, what he was supposed to do, but he had something else in mind. There was no reason he couldn't accomplish both his goals and the other mission at the same time.

He closed his eyes and imagined what her long dark hair would feel like in his hands. Would she smell like a sweet shampoo? The thought of touching her excited him greatly. What would she feel like underneath him? With him totally in control? He let the sound of her voice wash over him. As the commercial popped onto the TV screen, he cursed. It was too quick. When would he get to see her again? It would have to be soon. And of course, he also had other plans to attend to.

CHAPTER TWO

Viv made it through the first week unscathed. Gene was doing better and was soon going to be released from the hospital. But as the doctors told him, he'd be in heavy rest and recovery mode for months.

Viv sat at her desk in campaign headquarters and saw her favorite security hunk walking toward her. They hadn't talked much since their first run in, but she often saw him lurking around, giving her looks with those dark eyes.

"If it isn't the star spokesperson." He smiled and took a seat across from her.

"I don't know if star is the right word, but so far I haven't embarrassed myself or the campaign."

"It's getting late. Why don't you say we get out of here and let me buy you that drink?"

She looked up at him and grinned. "You're wasting your time, Marcus Locke."

"Why don't you let me decide for myself if it's a waste of time? No strings attached, I promise. Just a friendly get-to-know-you drink on a Friday night in DC. What can that hurt?"

God, she could think of a lot worse ways to spend a Friday night. She made up her mind she'd never let him take her home, but a couple of drinks wouldn't hurt her. After all, she deserved it. She'd already struck out with Serena who had plans with her hot mysterious boyfriend.

"All right. But just drinks."

A look of triumph flashed through his eyes. "Yes, ma'am. Just drinks." He leaned back casually in the chair and crossed his arms once again exposing his killer biceps. She hoped her approval wasn't obvious by her stare.

"So," he said. "Where does a girl like you enjoy having a drink?"

She started to speak, and he held up his hand. "Let me guess, somewhere like Spice? Or Cosmo Bar at the fancy Tower Hotel?"

Viv laughed loudly. "You wouldn't ever catch me in there, unless it was for a campaign fundraising event. I'm more of a chill bar scene type, and I love Irish pubs. Why don't we hit up Foley's?"

She could tell by his crooked smile that she'd surprised him, and she put one point in her column for the evening. Behind her fancy suit and polished exterior, she was a very simple girl who wasn't into the glitz and glam that was a necessary part of her job. When she got to unwind, she liked to do it her way.

"Foley's it is then. I'll leave my car here and we can walk to the Metro. It's only one stop down, right?"

"Yes. Another reason it's a good choice."

The hot summer air greeted them when they hit the sidewalk. She had on her high heels today so while she was still much shorter than him, it wasn't as bad as when they first met. She noticed that he kept a safe distance from her, and they didn't talk much on the Metro ride over, just the basics of their workday.

Since it was Friday night, Foley's was busy but not overpacked like many of the more trendy bars would be. They secured a booth, and Viv took off her suit jacket revealing a soft pink blouse. His eyes diverted to her chest for a brief moment. She wasn't surprised. He was a man after all. She tried to keep her curvy figure under wraps and was actually glad she got to wear a suit every day.

The server walked over. "What can I get you two?"

"I'll have your stout on draft," she said.

"Heck, you aren't playing around, huh? I'll have the same. Why don't we do a pitcher?"

She grinned. "You don't have to get stout. I know not everyone likes it. Get whatever you want."

He scoffed. "We'll have the stout." He narrowed his eyes at her.

She leaned back in her seat. "Fine, have it your way."

"I will." He challenged her.

She sighed and was ready for the beer to arrive. Marc unsettled her. It was his take charge military nature that already reminded her so much of her SEAL ex Scott. She had loved Scott, and Scott had loved her. But once he admitted to cheating on her, it was all over. Her trust in their relationship was broken forever. Even he understood that.

"You were in Florida before?" he asked.

"I was helping with our ground game operation there. It's a key swing state, so we've had our office down there since early on in the campaign. Gene wanted me to keep a close track on the media, especially in South Florida." After she said the last sentence she realized that she probably didn't need to be so open with him about strategy. Presumably he had signed confidentiality agreements, but that didn't stop some people. Abby's words about the nature of political campaigns rang loudly in her ears.

"How did you get involved with the Senator?"

The beer arrived, and she took a long slow drink before answering. "I interned for him while I was in college and getting my Master's."

"What's your Master's in?"

"REES," she said. "R-E-E-S."

"Acronyms. The military is great at those. Let me guess, you told me you speak Russia." He paused. "Russian and Eastern European studies?"

"Close. And I don't blame you since it doesn't exactly fit. Don't know why they left out one of the E's. It stands for Russian, Eurasian and Eastern European Studies."

Marc grabbed his beer mug and put it to his lips, then set it down. "Why didn't you go work for the State Department or intelligence or something? With that background, you would be a great asset."

She laughed. "Because obviously what I'm doing now isn't useful, right?" She raised her eyebrow.

He avoided eye contact for a moment and shifted in his seat. "Basically, yes. Politicians are their own special breed. If you really want to make a difference, you could do it elsewhere. And from the sound of it you really bring a lot to the table."

"What do you have against the Senator?" she asked. "You're in charge of his campaign security detail at headquarters. Doesn't that seem a bit odd?"

He shook his head. "Not in the least bit. I'm apolitical. I can assess threats, and provide security. I don't need to believe in a candidate for that. In fact, it's a lot better that I'm not emotionally involved. Keeps my head in the game."

Spoken like a true military guy. "How long did you serve?"

"Until I was thirty-two. Once I left, I started my own private security business. Seemed like the perfect fit for my skill set."

"Thirty-two isn't that old for the teams. Why didn't you stay longer?"

"You talk about the teams as if you know them?"

"My ex was a SEAL."

"Well why didn't you say so at first? That explains a lot." He grinned and took a swig of beer.

She couldn't help but like to see him smile. The way his large hands gripped the beer mug made her think about his hands on her body. *Stop,* she told herself. Yeah, she needed a hot night with a man, but not one like him. He could only be trouble.

Marc reached over and grabbed her hand. "I can guarantee you. I'm nothing like a SEAL."

His hand felt warm as it engulfed hers. The beer was impacting her thought process. She needed to order something to eat. And she needed to not get lost in those huge dark eyes that looked like they could devour her piece by piece. She'd enjoy every second of it. Then hate herself in the morning.

"How are you so different from a SEAL? Special Operations is Special Operations."

He made a dramatic pose and placed his hand over his heart. "Don't ever say that again. Delta Force is an entirely different breed of men. And don't forget the whole Army/Navy rivalry."

"If you say so." She shrugged and grabbed her mug which felt cold in contrast to his warm hand. The last thing she wanted to do was talk about her ex. That was a downer. "Can we talk about something else? The thought of my ex isn't doing it for me right now."

"That's my girl." He motioned for the server and ordered a second pitcher.

"Let's get some food too." After ordering burgers, she felt better knowing that food would be coming. She wanted to prove to him that she wasn't a light weight, so she didn't stop his second pitcher order. She just hoped he would drink faster than her.

She smiled and looked at him. "You know you skillfully avoided my original question. Maybe I should recruit you to the media team."

"What original question?" he asked trying to play innocent.

"Fine, I won't push it for now, but at some point maybe you'll tell me why you left the military. Why don't we talk about any security issues I need to be aware of?"

"Nothing so far. Between me and the Secret Service guys, we have everything well under control."

"I hope so."

She was grateful when the food arrived, and she took a huge bite of her burger.

"Have you dealt with Ralph from the Secret Service much?" Marc asked.

"Funny you ask. He actually swung by to see me this morning. He asked me out on a date for tomorrow night."

Marc coughed. "He did?"

"Yes." She enjoyed watching him squirm. She took a bite of a fry while he looked at her. For the first time since they'd met, he seemed to be at a loss for words.

"You shouldn't go. That guy is really a dog."

She laughed. "What, are you trying to protect my honor now?"

"Seriously, Viv."

There was something beneath the surface that let her know there was more about Ralph that he wasn't saying. "You can rest easy soldier. I turned him down."

"You did?"

"Yeah, I don't go for the blond, buff types."

He chuckled. "So what type do you go for?"

She was playing with fire. "The dark and dangerous type."

A flash of unmistakable heat went through his eyes. "Really? You like bad boys."

"Danger can come in many different forms. Unfortunately, my track record isn't very good." She pushed her plate away having finished her burger. Now she felt very relaxed as she eyed the second pitcher and noticed they were halfway through it.

"God, we're back to that ex of yours again aren't we? What did he do to you?"

She was put on the spot and felt her face redden. "Let's just say he may have been loyal to his teammates, but he certainly wasn't loyal to me." The wave of hurt and betrayal washed over her again. The thing that bothered her most was she never saw it coming.

Yeah, there was an inkling of doubt in her mind about whether he was "the one." But he never made her feel like he would cheat. It came as a complete shock. Then he didn't even try to stay in the relationship. He said it wasn't the honorable thing to do. After going through the anger and hurt phase, they had surprisingly become friends.

He grabbed her hand and gently rubbed. "You ready to get out of here?"

"Sure." Although she wasn't really ready for the night to end. She'd been having fun, but she knew it had to stop at some point.

She pulled out her wallet, and he reached over and touched her arm. "I asked you out for drinks. I'm an old fashioned kinda guy. It's on me."

"All right." She wasn't in the mood to put up a protest. He had invited her. The question was what did he have in mind next? They walked out of Foley's into the warm night air. "I'm going to cab it home. Best that I don't Metro it back to the office and drive right now. Last thing we need on the morning headlines— Senator's spokesperson pulled over for DUI."

He laughed and bumped into her shoulder gently. Then he put his arm around her. "Let me drive you. I'm good to drive."

Bad idea, she thought. Very bad idea. "Thanks for the offer, but it's probably best I take a cab."

"Don't be silly, Viv. I swear I'll drop you off and won't even try to worm myself inside your place." He paused and grinned. "Tonight at least."

She didn't trust herself. Not after the crazy week she'd had and the beer. "Thanks, but here's a cab right now." She hailed the passing taxi. Marc, ever the gentleman it seemed, opened the door for her and as she got in she quickly relayed her address and then promptly closed her eyes. That was close. Viv knew she was attracted to Marc, but it was a complication she didn't have the time to think about. Going for drinks was probably a bad idea, but one she didn't regret.

* * *

Marc kept replaying Friday night over and over in his head. Viv was really different than what he'd expected. He was surprised that she would want to drink stout at an Irish pub. It was contradictory to her totally put together, prim and proper appearance. And what an appearance it was. When she'd taken off that suit jacket, he'd gotten a look at her killer body, and he wasn't disappointed. But all of that was irrelevant. Yeah, she was a hot woman. He didn't have any problems getting hot women. His mission here was different. If he had to use some level of physical chemistry to get his evidence collected, he would. But he knew the boundaries. She would never suspect that he was working undercover for the FBI.

She was smart, no doubt. But he had the advantage of knowing all the information. One of the first things he wanted to determine was if she was in on this illegal campaign financing scheme or if she was a potential pawn.

His initial research verified what she told him Friday night. She'd interned for the Senator and had gotten a very impressive Master's degree at Georgetown. It still bothered him that she didn't actually put her skills to use for something good. All of her backstory was clean. Could she believe in the Senator so much that she'd be engaged in illegal activity to help him? That was exactly what he had to find out.

He'd been working this case ever since information was found that there was at least some coordination between a major Super Pac and Nelson's campaign. Under the law, these Super PACs could exist and pour tons of money into the campaign, but there was one big catch. They couldn't donate directly to the campaign, and the Super PACs couldn't coordinate with the campaign. It was a gray area at best.

But what *was* clear was the initial evidence. It showed a lot more than coordination. A heck of a lot more. There was one piece of evidence directly linking a Super PAC contribution to the Nelson campaign in exchange for Nelson taking a certain position on women's issues that the Super PAC wanted. He'd seen the email—the untraceable email. That sent off red flags at the FBI, but one contribution alone wasn't enough. They needed more to construct a powerful case. The campaign could come up with all kinds of excuses for one mistake—blame it in on the Super PAC. It was Marc's hunch, though, that if he kept digging he'd find a pattern. It wasn't his goal to help the President win re-election. He really didn't care who won, since he thought most politicians were corrupt or at least corruptible. He wouldn't stand by and watch a President get elected who he knew had engaged in illegal campaign practices. It was his job to find the truth, and then let the chips fall where they may.

Luckily for him, today was one of his first fundraising events working security and Viv would be there. The Secret Service would be on the Senator, so that gave Marc the perfect opportunity to investigate.

He walked into the large ballroom at the Four Seasons and could smell the money. It only took him a minute to spot Viv. She was all business in a dark brown pantsuit and her hair pulled back in a low sleek ponytail.

He saw the moment she recognized him. He took a few steps in her direction.

"You're working security?" she asked in a low tone.

"Yes, ma'am."

"It should be a pretty safe event. Which means boring for you. Just a ton of rich people eating and drinking and hopefully donating money. This event is hosted by our party so all the establishment types are here."

"What about Super PAC contributions?"

She looked at him with a raised eyebrow. "There shouldn't be any of that here today at this sanctioned event. Super PACs operate independently of the campaign and the party. That's why they can evade the personal contribution caps."

"Ah." He nodded.

"I didn't realize you were a campaign finance expert," she said with a hand on her hip.

"Oh, I'm not. Just hear a lot on the news about Super PACs. I didn't understand that distinction you were making. Thought it was just another part of fundraising."

She shook her head vigorously. "No. Definitely not. That's a hot button issue. We play by the book."

"Enough shop talk," he said. He didn't want to show his hand too much. "What about grabbing another drink sometime?"

Viv cocked her head to the side, and her blue eyes flashed with warmth. And he hoped interest. "Let me think about it, all right?"

"I'll take that. You working this thing until the bitter end?"

"No, I have to go back now to the office and do some media follow up via email."

"I have to be here for a bit longer to work my shift. Maybe I'll see you later tonight or, if not, tomorrow."

She smiled and walked away leaving him wanting more. A lot more. She told a good story about playing by the book, but he knew better than to take that at face value. What, was she just going to tell the security consultant, "Yeah, we're taking illegal Super Pac money?" Yeah, right. But maybe she would confide in him if he got closer to her. He'd keep pushing.

* * *

Viv was exhausted by the time she got back to headquarters. She slid off her heels and massaged her aching feet which hurt almost as much as her head. It had been another long day, and the days were only going to get longer. She couldn't help that tingling feeling in her stomach that she got from seeing Marc again. He was proving to be quite persistent. How much will power did she have?

There was something behind those dark eyes and dazzling smile she couldn't quite put her finger on. A little mystery or maybe it was just a whole lotta heat. And she was going through a dry spell. The campaign had really taken a toll on her love life. She worked and worked, and loved every second of it. But a little attention from a man would be nice. Nothing serious, she didn't need attachments. Just a fun fling. Men had flings all the time, so why couldn't she?

Headquarters was relatively quiet as a lot of staff was still at the fundraising event. But one of the volunteers walked over to her desk carrying a vase of flowers.

"Viv, someone delivered these for you tonight."

"Thanks," she said. She looked at the flowers. Would Marc have really sent them? The purple lilacs were stunning and a very interesting choice. She opened the card. It simply said: *Can't wait to see you again.*

Of course Marc knew he'd be seeing her again since they worked together in the same building. There was nothing else on the card. How strange. She sat down at her desk and stared at the flowers. What kind of game was he playing?

She couldn't dwell on the flowers right now. She'd just have to ask him about it. He certainly didn't seem like the wooing type. Viv got lost in her email, responding to requests for quotes from various media outlets. She was starting to get in her groove when a hand on her shoulder made her jump.

Viv looked up and saw Marc. "Hey, I thought you'd still be at the event."

"I was. It's almost midnight. I came here to lock down the place."

"I lost track of time." Viv ran her hand through her hair that she'd taken out of the ponytail. "I got wrapped up in emails and promotional media. Got a few more national spots on primetime shows this week. Pretty exciting."

"Congratulations." Marc smiled and shifted his weight to one side, leaning up against her desk. "Nice flowers. Where did you get those?" He nodded toward the vase. "Very vibrant."

She laughed. "Do you always take such pride in gloating about your own gifts? That's a new one." She leaned back in her chair.

"What do you mean? I'd love to take credit, but I didn't send you those."

"Are you sure?" She paused. "You'd fess up right?"

"I'd want the credit if I sent them. Then I'd be sure to get another round of drinks with you."

"Well, who sent them then?" She pulled the card out.

"Let me see it." He gently took the card from her hand.

"See, it says can't wait until I see you again. And has no signature."

He flipped the card down on her desk. "It must be Ralph. You turned him down. Now he sees you as a real challenge. So he decided to start trying to put on the hard sell."

"You think so? I wouldn't have pegged him that way. It's kinda cute."

"Remember what I told you about him, Viv. I'd stay away from him. No matter how nice the flowers are he sends you." He leaned down close to her ear, and she could feel his warm breath on her neck. "I promise I'd treat you better than that guy. Let's get you out of here. It's late."

She looked at the clock again confirming the late hour and rose from her chair. He put his hand on her lower back, and she could feel the hot electricity pulsing through her body. She didn't even complain or try to back away when he walked her to the lot behind the headquarters.

"Which car is yours?"

"I'm the hybrid compact."

He laughed. "I should've known. I probably couldn't even get half my body in your car."

"Well you're a tall guy. If you haven't noticed, I'm a bit on the small side."

The lights from the parking area were dim, but she could see him grin.

He reached out and grabbed her hand. "Believe me, I've noticed, and more than just your height."

"Really," she said, as she leaned against her car door.

He dropped his head down closer to hers, and she thought he was going to kiss her. But instead he whispered in her ear. "Let me know about that drink. I can bring you flowers tomorrow if that would sway you."

"Maybe I'll have you and Ralph fight it out." She laughed but his expression was serious.

"Good night, Viv. See you tomorrow."

"Good night."

As she drove home, she was feeling guilty for wanting him to kiss her. Scott had really done a number on her confidence when it came to men. She second guessed herself now in ways she didn't before. And more than anything, she didn't want to get duped a second time. It wasn't worth the risk taking a chance on love with a guy like Marc right now.

She was her own woman after all the years of struggling alone to make something of herself. Her parents' deaths seemed fresh even though it had been many years. She hadn't worked and fought her way through to get her dream job to be distracted now by a guy. She'd have to find a way to put distance in between her and Marc. Or else.

CHAPTER THREE

Marc took a few minutes to surf the net to check baseball scores. He needed a break as he kept running into dead ends. He hadn't been able to find any additional evidence through all of his research. Even given his great access to the campaign, he was coming up short. Peter wouldn't be happy that his investigation was moving so slowly. He was wound up and the afternoon was dragging on. His cell chirped loudly. He looked down and was surprised to see Viv's name. He had programmed her into his phone as part of his campaign contacts, but never really expected to see her number appear.

"Hello," he answered. He leaned back in a chair at campaign headquarters.

"Marc?"

"Yes, ma'am." He smiled at the sound of her voice.

"It's Viv. Don't freak out."

"Uh oh. I don't like the sound of that. What's going on?" He tensed preparing for the unknown.

"I came home early this afternoon from my media rounds, and there was an envelope on my door. I didn't think much of it. Thought it was more spam advertising. But when I opened it, there was a message inside."

He could hear her faint breathing on the other side of the phone. "What kind of message?"

"'It said I can't wait to see you. Just like those flowers. But it also said…" She paused. "I've been watching you.'"

Marc sat up straight in his chair. Not only was this bad, it also distracted him from his main mission. But right now, his first concern was Viv's safety. "Don't move. Are you still at home?"

"Yes," she said softly.

"Give me your address." He already had it, but he couldn't tell her that. He wrote down the information anyway. "I'll be right there, okay?"

"Are you going to tell Ralph?"

"Yes, I have to since he's technically the head of the Nelson campaign's security, but not this minute. Hang tight and make sure your doors are locked."

He cursed as he quickly jogged out of the campaign headquarters. First the flowers and now the note. What was more troubling was that the note was left at her house, not headquarters. Ralph wasn't behind this. It looked like Viv had picked up a stalker. Given her multiple national TV appearances, he couldn't say he was shocked. She was a good looking woman who quite a few sickos might have an interest in, but this could be larger than just that. He had no idea. He also didn't know whether this was just a pathetic admirer or something more sinister.

By the time he'd reached her condo, he was in full Delta mode—strategizing his plan of attack. He walked up to her door and knocked. "Viv, it's Marc," he said, making sure to identify himself. He surveyed her street. Viv lived in a safe Arlington neighborhood. A woman walked her dog. Kids were playing with a soccer ball in her neighbor's yard. Definitely not a bad area of town.

The door eased open and there she stood. She'd changed out of her usual suit and into a snug fit t-shirt and jeans. God, she looked amazing.

"C'mon in," she said.

He walked into her condo and stepped into the living room. Not surprisingly, her place looked spotless. The living room had an average size TV and comfortable looking L shaped couch. A furry calico cat sat on the couch, eyeing him with guarded suspicion.

"Nice place." He looked around and walked toward the kitchen area. He could smell coffee.

"Thanks. It's not big, but it's perfect for me and Willow."

Ah, the cat, he thought. "Willow doesn't look too happy for me to be here."

"She's skeptical of men and rightfully so. My ex claimed he was allergic so he treated her like she had the plague. I think it was just a stupid excuse to ignore her because he didn't like cats."

"Luckily for you, I love animals. Even ones that look at me like they'd like to claw my eyeballs out." He turned his attention away from the cat and back to her. She looked fine, but he could sense a little bit of nerves floating off of her as he watched her breathing.

"Where's the note?" He took a step toward her.

She pointed to the kitchen table. He pulled some gloves out of his pocket that he snagged from a med kit before leaving the campaign headquarters. He picked up the letter. He figured there wouldn't be prints if the guy knew what he was doing, but they might be dealing with an amateur so he didn't want to take any chances. He examined the envelope and then the blue note with the strangely perfect handwriting. Control. This guy was a control freak.

What concerned him most was the last line. Yeah, he could mean watching her on TV. But he was at her house for God's sake. He might be watching her in person. "We'll need to send this to the lab for testing. I'll have to turn it over to Ralph and let the Secret Service guys decide if they want to run it federally or have locals get involved. But I'd say between the flowers and the note on your door, you've got a stalker."

She crossed her arms and bit her bottom lip. "I'm sure it's just some stupid guy with too much time on his hands. Right?"

"I don't want you to get too worried, but we have no idea what we're dealing with. Could be that, or could be this guy is a danger to you and maybe even to the Senator. That's why we have to get Ralph involved."

She sighed deeply her shoulders visibly dropping as she sat down at the kitchen table. "Well, this sucks."

"Between me and Ralph and his guys, we'll keep you safe."

"I've got a job to do. I can't be looking over my shoulder every five minutes. We're in the middle of a presidential campaign. "

He took a seat at the table across from her and reached over and grabbed her hand. "We got this. I promise."

She didn't look convinced.

"Let's talk about your daily routine. Are you consistent?"

She propped her chin up in her hand with her elbow on the table. "What do you mean?"

"Coming and going. Do you usually leave at a certain time? Do you do anything outside, like jogging? I'm trying to figure out your patterns."

"Things have really been in flux since I took over as campaign spokesperson. The schedule is never exactly the same with all the media appearances. I usually leave here by eight to go into head-quarters. But if I'm doing events or other media, I may go to the site directly, and the times vary greatly."

He nodded his head. "I understand."

"I do run outside. Not every morning. But if I do, I go around six or so. It's not light out when I start. I also have a treadmill for days when it's gross out."

"Okay, jogging outside is going to need to stop for the time being. Stick to your treadmill."

"I'm already not liking these adjustments. Why don't we put some type of surveillance camera outside?"

"That will work if he's stupid. If he's smart, he knows that once he put this letter on your door, we could do just that. He'll be a lot more careful from now on, but I agree that's a reasonable step."

She blew out a breath and looked at him with those sparkling blue eyes. His protective streak was showing. He could feel it, and he noticed how she was downplaying this incident. But he still had a job to do, two jobs rather: protecting campaign members on top of his own investigation. It was a good thing Ralph was in charge. Probably better in the long run to have Ralph worry about her anyway. He needed to focus on gathering intel. But as he looked at her, he knew he couldn't just pretend like nothing was happening.

"So, what now?" she asked.

"I need to call Ralph."

"Now?" she asked, seemingly hesitant.

"Yes."

She groaned and walked over to the fridge. "Do you want a drink?"

"Sure."

"I feel like this day calls for something stronger than my usual offerings. Beer or liquor?"

"A beer would be good. Let me guess, you have some fancy stout hiding in there?" He was trying to lighten the mood.

She smiled and leaned back against the refrigerator propping one foot behind her. "I am very well equipped."

He couldn't help but think about how well equipped she was in all areas. Her dark hair was loose and hanging down past her shoulders. She looked amazingly sexy, and he wished he could have her. Things had only gotten more complicated tonight.

"Surprise me then. I've never found a beer I didn't like."

She reached into the fridge and pulled out a German wheat beer. He was liking her more and more. The last thing she seemed like right now was a corrupt political insider. She looked more like the girl next door.

"Can you just give me a few minutes to have a drink before you call Ralph?"

"Sure." He liked that she obviously preferred him to Ralph. It was an ego thing.

"I knew things were going too smoothly."

"Yeah, this wasn't exactly what I had in mind when I asked you for drinks again. But I'll take it."

She grinned and took a sip of her beer.

"Do you have any media events tomorrow?"

"Yeah, a couple. Also have to make an appearance at another fundraiser."

Great, she just provided him with another opportunity to do some much-needed research. "I thought you didn't do that much with those."

"I put in the required face time. We have our whole fundraising team that devotes their life to that twenty four seven."

"Who's in charge of that?"

"Fundraising director is Carl Wells, but Arthur has his hand in everything."

"Yeah, I got that feeling. He can be a bit pushy."

She laughed. "Yeah, and he isn't in love with the idea of me keeping this job. He'd rather put one of his old school cronies in front of the cameras. But the Senator and Abby have been happy with the results so far. We got some favorable traction in the latest tracking polls. I really think I can help with the female demographic. I've worked hard for Senator Nelson, so I'm not going to let Arthur try to stand in my way."

"What's his deal?"

"He's hypercompetitive. He's one of those people that live for campaigns. I enjoy the campaign, but I'm more about the candidate, and what will actually happen post the campaign. Policy making. Making a difference. But with him, he enjoys the gamesmanship. It drives him. And he does not like to lose."

"Sounds like he'd do anything to win."

"Almost." She took another long sip of beer and then licked her lips.

Her lips. He wondered if she was trying to tempt him on purpose. Regardless, he was tempted. He wanted to go pull her out of that chair and press his body against hers. What would she do if he tried to make a move? He couldn't tell. Maybe baby steps.

He reached over and took her hand again. She didn't flinch and made eye contact. He ran his thumb across her hand. Her skin was as soft as he'd imagined it. He let go of her hand and then stood up. Walking behind her chair, he started massaging her shoulders.

"You seem tense. Thought you might like me to try to work out the kinks."

She groaned, and he took that as a yes to keep going. Her shoulders were small, and his hands felt so good on her body. He felt her have a little chill, and he knew she couldn't deny the attraction between them.

It would be too easy to start kissing down her neck and tell her how good he could make her feel. She was letting him in a little bit and now wasn't the time to push it. She could be the key to breaking his case wide open—either by her direct involvement or her knowledge. He couldn't let go of his control now.

She sighed again, and he took a step back from her chair. "We should probably call Ralph now."

She turned around and looked up at him. "I guess so."

A spark of disappointed floated through her blue eyes for a brief second before he saw worry crease her brow. The second gesture was enough to let him know he'd made the right call. Regardless of how hard it was. Or how hard he was for that matter.

He picked up his phone and dialed Ralph.

"This is Major," Ralph said.

"It's Marc. We've got an issue."

"What type of issue?" he asked sharply.

"I'm over at Viv's condo. Someone left a note on her door. Probably the same guy who sent her flowers. I think she might have a stalker, but I'll explain it all when you get here. You need to come take a look."

"Give me the address. I'll be right there."

Marc provided him the address.

"You're staying with her until I get there, right?"

"Of course."

"I have a bad feeling about this."

"I hear you."

***

Viv poured herself another drink. Ralph and Marc went off into the living room and were talking in hushed tones. She didn't like it one bit. They were obviously trying to keep her out of the loop of whatever they were cooking up. She knew it was necessary to involve the Secret Service, but she didn't have to be enthused by it.

"Okay guys," she said loudly. "I'm in here you know."

After a minute they both walked back in with serious looks on their faces. Marc looked mildly annoyed as he narrowed his eyes at her. She didn't know what his problem was.

Ralph had lost that easy look she often saw in his blue eyes. "I've called this in to my core team. We'll have the letter tested and see if we can pull anything off of it. I also think I need to alert the Senator, but I need to consult with my guys."

"No," she stepped in. "Why do we need to bother him over this? He has so much on his plate right now."

"I'm sorry, Viv. It's standard operating procedure. More than likely this guy is just some nut job who thinks you're attractive and wants to make a play. But he could be much more dangerous than that. After my team evaluates the threat, we'll make a final determination as to whether the Senator should be notified."

She felt defeated. Arthur could use this as an excuse to remove her. He certainly would. The campaign wouldn't want the possible negative attention. She started pacing around the room. "What if the media hears about this? It wouldn't be good for the campaign and would only serve as a distraction."

Marc took a step forward. "Maybe she's right. The last thing we need is for the press to get wind of this and sensationalize it. That could lead to copy cats and mass chaos."

"I understand that," Ralph replied. "Which is why this is only on a Secret Service need to know basis right now. But if we determine there is an increased risk after we do our assessment, then the Senator will have to be brought in along with the rest of the staff."

She was fighting a losing battle. "Just do what you have to do."

Ralph reached over and gently patted her shoulder. "We haven't even discussed the most important issue right now."

"Which is?"

"Your own personal security."

"What do you mean?"

"Marc and I have talked about it, and while I'm taking lead on the investigation, we think it would be a good idea for him to assist you with your personal security issues."

What the heck was Ralph talking about? "I don't have any personal security issues." She pushed her hair back off her shoulders. "What I have is some nice flowers and a creepy note. Until there's additional reason to worry about my individual safety, I'm going to go about my life."

"And we want you to," Marc added. "But I will be providing you with additional security."

She turned to Ralph. "The Secret Service is signing off on this?"

"Yes, ma'am. It's a good solution. Marc's company specializes in personal security services. My team will focus on the investigation. I promise you, we'll track him down."

Ralph no longer seemed like the annoying guy trying to get into bed with her. He finally seemed like a Secret Service agent on a mission.

Ralph reached over and touched her shoulder again. "I'll let you and Marc best figure out how you want to handle things for now. I'll take the evidence in for processing. If you need anything at any time, don't hesitate to call me, all right?"

She nodded. "Yes. Thanks."

Ralph tipped his head to Marc and then walked out of the condo leaving her alone with Marc. For a moment, neither of them spoke.

"I can tell you don't seem too happy about this."

"I think you two are overacting. Guys can be crazy."

"But you understand why it has to be this way?"

"Not really. I don't think that I have any real personal security issues, or whatever it is you want to call them."

"Listen, Viv." He took a step, closing the distance between them. "If this guy is dangerous, then you could be in real trouble. This could be a big threat. Yeah, it might be nothing, but we're not in a position to make that call. The call will be made by Ralph. This is his gig. I'm second on the list, not first. Private security guys like me don't play the same role as the Secret Service. They're calling the shots."

"I take it by the sound of your voice you don't like that. I guess it's hard for a Delta guy like you to take a backseat."

"Of course it is. And I never said I was taking a backseat. Just that I couldn't make the decisions. I plan to do my job, and part of that job is protecting you."

"What do you suggest?" She shifted her weight to one side and put her hand on her hip. "I hope you don't think this is an easy way to get into my house and then into my bed."

His eyes lit up a bit, and he laughed. "Nothing about being in bed with me would be easy. And no. When I want to get you into bed, I won't need to use any guise."

A chill shot down her back at his statement. She'd been around alpha males before but none quite as confident as Marc. It was incredibly attractive. Even as she tried to keep her face passive, inside she was on fire. Her pulse was racing, and she was almost sure she was blushing.

"All right, tough guy. We'll play it your way for now. What do we do?"

"Unless you agree to around the clock security which I'm assuming you won't?"

She shook her head.

"As I figured. We need to be in constant contact. Regular check-ins. I need full access to your schedule each day—where you're going, who you're with. All of that. No detail is too trivial for me. I need you to be more alert. As I told you before, no jogging outside. If you want to run, let me know, I'll be happy to go with you. But for now, it's not safe for you to be out by yourself like that. I'd prefer that either I or someone else is with you for all of your appearances."

"This is pretty extreme. I'm the campaign spokesperson." She felt her voice elevating. "How can I do my job?"

"It might be overkill, but it's our play right now. We can adjust strategy as needed if we find out something that changes our thoughts on who this guy is."

"What's your working theory?" she asked. "Because I'm sure you already have one, right?"

"I think he's becoming obsessed with you. With each TV spot, he feels like he knows you more and more. And he wants you more and more. It would be pure speculation for me to posit if there's any connection to the Senator, or if it's just you. But I lean to the ladder. You're a beautiful woman. I'm not surprised that there's a psycho out there who would latch on to you."

"What if he's not a psycho, but just some guy who's interested in me?"

"Okay, maybe if it was just the flowers, then I could give you that. But the last sentence of the note kills that for me. I mean, I get it. Men are idiots. But most of us realize that creepy-sounding notes are not the way to a woman's heart—or to her bed."

She shivered thinking about the possibility that this guy was dangerous. Marc's eyes warmed, and he put his strong arm around her. Then he pulled her close, and she could smell a hint of his masculine cologne. He fully engulfed her with his much larger body. With his arms wrapped around her, she felt safe.

"I'm going to take good care of you, Viv. You can count on that."

"I don't doubt you. It's just a lot to comprehend. I was so excited earlier today. I'd gotten such great reviews, and everything seemed to be going well. Then this happened. Wish I would've trashed that envelope as junk mail without even opening it."

He released her and took a step back. "It wouldn't have mattered. He would've just sent something else. When is your next TV spot?"

"Tomorrow."

"Is it from headquarters or on site?"

"On site," she said.

"I'd like to go with you. I swear I won't follow you everywhere, but I'd feel better shadowing you."

"That's fine." What was she doing? She knew better than to allow him so much access into her life, but here she was. And now all she wanted to think about was him pulling her back into his arms and kissing her. She needed a fling. Badly. And now more than ever she knew that Marc was not the right man for that.

"Good, sounds like a plan."

She looked down at her watch. "I'm starving, and I have nothing here."

"Want to go out and get something? I'll drive, and we won't talk anything about this. You need to get your mind off of it at least for tonight."

"Food would be great."

"You didn't hit the whiskey while I was talking to Ralph did you?" He nodded in direction of the whiskey bottle sitting on the table.

"Just one shot."

He lightly punched her in the arm. "You're a serious drinker."

"One shot of whiskey and a beer is not serious." She laughed. "You should see me when I really throw down."

A slow grin spread across his face. "Now, I would love to see that. Just let me know when you're ready to throw down and I'm game."

"Wait, I wasn't challenging you to anything. I know how you military guys are about challenges. You probably have a hundred pounds, or so, on me."

He chuckled. "Yeah, don't worry about that. I wouldn't expect you to be able to keep up with me. If you did, I would be worried you had a serious drinking problem."

She smiled at his joke and felt his hand on the small of her back.

"Anything else to do before we go?" she asked.

"Just this," he said, as he leaned down and pressed his warm lips to hers.

* * *

God, she tasted good. He only allowed himself a moment to enjoy it before he broke away. Her eyes widened and he watched as she cocked her head to the side, seemingly asking him what the heck that was for.

"Let's go eat." He opened the door, and she walked through it. Maybe he could use this stalker development to ask more questions of her than he normally would. He hoped he would have opportunities to do so, but tonight he'd keep things light.

"Where are we going?" She slid into the passenger seat of his truck.

"How do you feel about Thai food? There's a hole in the wall place that has the best Thai in town."

"Oh," she moaned. The sound of her voice almost killed him. "I love Thai food. The spicier the better."

"Another thing we have in common then."

They were seated in a quiet booth as the restaurant was almost empty. They didn't waste any time placing their orders.

"Tell me more about you, Viv."

"I grew up in Florida. I'm an only child. Went to Georgetown for undergrad and grad school."

"What about your parents? Where do they live?"

"They were killed in a car accident the summer before I started at Georgetown."

"I'm sorry, Viv."

"It's all right. I managed on my own. Definitely required me to grow up a lot faster than I had planned. College wasn't all fun and games for me. I had to work really hard to make sure I kept my scholarship."

"I can't even imagine how tough that would've been for you."

"It made me the person I am today. Enough about me. What about you?"

"I'm from everywhere. My dad was in the military so we constantly moved around. Also lived in Germany for a bit. I went to West Point, and then the rest is history."

She laughed. "Not exactly. You're leaving a lot out from being in the military to ending up on Delta Force."

"It's a long story, and a lot of it is classified."

She smiled and tapped her fingers on the table. "That won't deter me. I can be very persistent. Part of my job."

He leaned back and thought about how much he could or should tell her. Opening up would further their relationship, and that's what he needed right now. He obviously couldn't tell her the full truth. Did he even know it?

"I went into Army Special Forces first, basically what you would know as the Green Berets. After two years as a Green Beret, I transitioned to Delta."

"I have to admit, I don't know much about Delta. I'm a bit more familiar with the SEALs."

"And you wouldn't be familiar. Everything about Delta is highly classified. The SEALs are out there more in popular culture. Operators for Delta just want to get the job done."

"Operators?"

"Inside Delta, we're known as Operators. It's a distinction we like to make. We're not like the regular military or soldiers. Delta is different." That was an understatement. Delta had more secrets too. He knew he had enough of his own. Like losing his best friend when times got tough.

The hot plates of noodles, rice, and spring rolls appeared in front of them, and they started digging in. He was impressed that she had no problem loading up on noodles and spring rolls.

"That's so interesting. My ex loved telling me SEAL stories." She licked the spicy peanut sauce away from her lips, and he felt himself losing his focus. "The funny thing is I think he was making most of it up. They were so outlandish, and I knew he couldn't tell me real events so he had to change those details anyway."

"This guy seems like a piece of work. Would love to meet him."

"Don't get me wrong. I have no doubt that he was great at his job. I didn't have any concerns about his dedication to the teams. But he didn't have that same dedication to me. At least not as a girlfriend."

"So now you're written off all military guys forever?"

A stray hair fell out of her low ponytail, and she pushed it back. "I'd be stupid to make that same mistake twice. Let's just say I'm going to be a lot more cautious in the future. And right now men are the last thing on my to-do list. If you haven't noticed, I have a presidential campaign to win." She smiled.

"I don't think I'm anything like your ex."

She leaned back, and her eyes seemed even bluer tonight. She gave him a hard look as if trying to figure him out.

"I asked you the other day, but you skillfully evaded my answer." She twirled some noodles on her fork, and he knew what was coming. "Why did you leave the military?"

"It was time. I'd done a lot, been through a lot. My body was so beat up. I didn't recover as quickly as I did when I was younger. It just seemed right." He stuck to the story he'd told many times and tried to make it sound like the truth. Nothing could have been further from it. He felt a little bad lying to her, but it was all for the greater good.

"You seem like you're in fine shape to me."

"Looks can be deceiving." He heard the words come out before he had a chance to stop himself.

"I agree with that. People misjudge me all the time." She leaned forward. "Admit it. You probably thought I was some half-brained bimbo when we first met."

"Not quite half-brained." He laughed.

She poked her fork into a spring roll and took a bite. "Very funny."

"I try."

She sighed. "I know we said we weren't going to talk about my issue."

"But?"

"Tell me, honestly. No bullshitting. Do you really think I should be afraid?"

He took a moment, choosing his words carefully this time. "Should you live in fear? No. Should you be more careful? Absolutely. Will I be around more? Yes. If nothing else happens, then fine. But if this guy pops back up, which I bet he will, then we'll be ready. Also there wasn't much time lag between first and second contact. Which tells me you'll hear from him again soon."

"So we'll meet at headquarters in the morning, and then you'll go with me to my appearances?"

"Yes, ma'am."

"The ma'aming is quite cute."

"Thank you, ma'am."

She grinned, and he felt the warm heat of their attraction flow through him again.

"So, what did you think of Ralph tonight?" she asked.

"What do you mean?"

"He actually seemed like a real professional instead of a meathead."

"He knows his stuff. Just because I said you shouldn't go out with him doesn't mean he's not good at his job."

"Does it bother you that they're taking the lead?"

"Yes," he answered without hesitation. "I hate deferring, but here we are. I obviously got the better end of this assignment. Security detail on you is infinitely better than just tracking this wacko."

"And why is that?"

"Because I'll have more time to convince you that I'm not like that jerk ex of yours. And you'll come round to the idea of hanging out with me."

"There's that confidence again."

"Where are we going tomorrow for your TV gig?"

"CBW News."

"Wow, I'm impressed. That's a big outlet."

Her eyes lit up with excitement. "I know, right? I can't be off my game. We should get back to my place so I can try to get a few hours of sleep."

He patted her hand in as friendly a way as he knew how. "You ready?"

"Yeah."

Once back at the condo, he did a thorough room by room security sweep to satisfy himself that everything was indeed okay. Nothing was going to happen to Viv on his watch. He was most intrigued by her bedroom. Once he saw it, he clearly could see her design influence matched what he had gotten to know about her so far. The room was decorated in ivory and beige with a hint of gold. It was feminine without being frilly—just like Viv. The cat followed him around closely as he went room to room. He stopped before looking at a bedroom that Viv used as an office. "Cat, what do you have against me, huh?"

"Talking to Willow?"

Her voice actually startled him. He was too intent on having that conversation with the damn cat.

"Yeah." He laughed. "I don't know why she hates me so much. She hissed at me when I went in your bathroom."

"She thinks everything here is hers. Which means, you're improperly invading her turf."

"Maybe she'll get used to me with time."

"That assumes you're going to be here a lot."

He winked. "I like that assumption."

"You all done?"

"Yes, ma'am. Everything is secure here. You'll lock yourself in and set the alarm when I leave, right?"

"Yes, sir," she said mockingly.

"I'm serious."

"I will."

"See you in the morning, Viv. Sweet dreams."

CHAPTER FOUR

Viv was running, but she couldn't get away. He was closing in on her and fast. She screamed, but no one could hear her. She could feel his hot breath burning down her neck. His hands gripped her ankles, and she fell hard into the flames. The heat engulfed her entire body singing her skin.

Viv sat up in the bed trying desperately to catch her breath. God, that was an awful nightmare. She looked over at the clock, and saw it was just two a.m. Sweat poured down her back. When was the last time she'd had a dream like that? It had been a while, and the last thing she wanted was for those dreams to come back. After the car crash that had killed her parents, she'd battled nightmares for two years. It was a familiar feeling that she wanted to shake.

She looked over at Willow sleeping peacefully snuggled on the pillow beside her. She was on edge. Would she even be able to go back to sleep? Maybe a snack or drink would help. She walked toward the kitchen but when she got to the bedroom door, she heard a noise. Was she imagining things? She stopped and listened. There it was again. A rattling noise, coming from the living room. She took a step being as quiet as she could be. Then she heard the sound again. Someone was trying to come in through her back patio door. Crap. What was she going to do?

She raced back into her room, deciding between dialing 911, or Marc. She made the split second decision to call Marc. As it was ringing, she hit the panic button on her home alarm, sending a blaring noise. Hopefully that would scare the guy away. Now was a time she wished she wasn't so staunchly against having a weapon in her house.

"Viv. Viv, are you there? Answer me dammit." She heard Marc's voice on the other end of the phone.

"Yes, someone is trying to break into my back door. I just hit the panic button on the alarm."

"Get as far away from that door as possible. You hear me?"

"Yes." She tried to answer calmly, but her hands were shaking. Her whole body felt numb from fear.

"I'm on my way."

"I don't hear anything now. I think I scared him away."

"Probably so, but whatever you do, don't go looking around outside. Promise me."

"I promise."

Viv sat on her bed wanting to crawl into a ball and hide. She pulled Willow onto her lap and held her close. What if he was still outside trying to get in? He had to have left, right?

She waited for what felt like an eternity. Then Marc called and let her know he was there. She went to the front door to let him in.

He walked through the door with fire in his dark eyes. "I never should have left you here tonight. Are you okay?"

"Yes. Just a bit shaken up. I wouldn't have even heard him if I hadn't been awake. I couldn't sleep and was about to walk to the kitchen, and that's when I heard the patio door rattling."

He nodded. "There's always a chance this could be a break in attempt not connected to the stalker, but those odds are about one in a million. This isn't a high crime area."

"The police should be on their way because the alarm automatically sends them an instant notification."

"I need to loop Ralph in ASAP. He'll want to take point on this." He pulled out his phone. He punched the keypad but then walked over and put his other arm around her. Just feeling the warmth of his strong muscular body against hers made her feel safe. This situation was escalating quickly. Flowers and notes were one thing. Someone trying to break into her house, and do God knows what, was completely different. She shivered and felt his grip tighten around her.

"Ralph. We have another situation at Viv's. Need you back over here now."

She couldn't hear what Ralph said, but it was short because Marc pocketed his phone. Then he put his other arm around her and pulled her close in a hug.

"What would've happened if he would've gotten in?" she whispered.

"Don't think in terms of what ifs. It'll drive you crazy. The important thing is that he didn't, and you're safe."

She took in his words and his embrace. A knock at the door made her jump.

"I'm sure it's local PD," Marc said, but he protectively went to the door himself. "Yeah, it's them."

Viv walked into the kitchen and sat down. She could hear Marc's calm and no-nonsense voice as he discussed what happened with the police officers after they apologized for being delayed by a bad accident. Then she heard Ralph's voice. It was obvious to her that Ralph was about to send the cops on their way without even talking to her. She was fine with that. It wasn't like the local police could do anything to help her.

She heard the door shut, and then Ralph and Marc murmuring in such low voices she couldn't make out what they were saying. She'd had enough sitting and waiting, so she walked to the living room where they stood talking.

"You guys are doing it again. I think I deserve to know what's going on here."

They both turned and looked at her with scowls on their faces.

Ralph walked over. "Viv, this situation is no longer a little annoyance. You could've gotten hurt. I called the Senator on my way over."

"Tonight? It's what, three a.m.?"

"This kind of thing couldn't wait. We are going to up his security detail stat, and you need your own security which Marc is going to cover. Until we catch this guy, we can't take any chances."

"So what does all that mean?"

"My team is on their way. The locals dusted for prints, but we're going to go behind them. Also do a perimeter check to see if anything is out of the ordinary. And until this is over, Marc is going to be your shadow."

She shivered, this time not from fear, but from the idea of being around Marc so much.

"I guess we're all up for the remainder of the night. I'll make some coffee."

"Thanks, Viv. And once again, we're not going to let you down," Ralph said.

Viv walked back to the kitchen followed by Marc.

"There was sure a lot of whispering going on in there between you two," she said. She grabbed the coffee down from the cabinet and filled up the pot with water.

"Nothing for you to be worried about. More logistics. It's a touchy issue with the Secret Service and the locals involved, plus me. And then, of course, we are right in the middle of a presidential campaign. Given that the first debate is right around the corner, the media attention is only going to increase."

"You think this is going to get out?"

"Ralph is going to do his best to keep the local cops to keep their mouths shut, but there can be no guarantees."

"And I guess this means no keeping it from the rest of the campaign staffers."

"Everyone will be put on a higher level of alert." He reached over and grabbed her hand. "Your hands are cold. Do you need to put on more clothes?"

For the first time all night, she looked down and realized all she had on was a tank top and shorts. "Uh, maybe." All a sudden, she felt self-conscious as she crossed her arms over her chest. "Let me go grab a sweatshirt. I had the air conditioning up too high. I was hot earlier."

She went to her bedroom and found her favorite Georgetown sweatshirt. This all felt like a nightmare. Maybe she'd never woken up from the dream. Could this really be happening to her?

She walked back into the kitchen, and Marc handed her a mug of coffee. "Didn't know how you took yours."

"Thanks," she said. The warm mug felt great around her hands. She reached in the fridge and got out some flavored creamer seeking comfort in the rich sweetness. She wasn't in the mood to drink black coffee.

The Secret Service guys had arrived and were milling about. How was she going to do her interview in a few hours? She probably looked like death warmed over. She'd need a lot of help in the makeup department.

Now was time to settle in and get through the next couple of hours. And hope for a better day.

* * *

Marc met Peter first thing in the morning at the coffee shop. Ralph had offered to stay with Viv while he went home to get some things. But in addition he had to fill Peter in on what was going on. Events on the ground were changing rapidly.

Peter took a huge bite of a bagel and nodded to Marc, prodding him to start talking.

"We have a situation, sir."

"I already don't like the sound of this."

"The new campaign spokesperson, Vivian Reese. It seems she has a stalker." Marc took a sip of his coffee. Today was going to be caffeine overload day.

"What does that mean?" Peter narrowed his eyebrows.

"She received some flowers at headquarters and a note on her door at home. And then last night someone, presumably this wacko, tried to break into her house."

"Shit."

"Yeah, it definitely makes our investigation more complicated. The Secret Service has tasked me with keeping her safe."

"And what about your cover? Is it still good?"

"Yes, perfectly intact. That's not the issue. But this means I can't let anything happen to her. Can you imagine the headlines if it got out that I was there undercover and something happened on the FBI's watch?"

Peter's eyes darkened. "You cannot let that happen."

"Understood, sir. This will give me an opportunity to deepen the investigation, by gaining her trust and figuring out if she knows anything we could use."

"Do you think she's involved in the illegal contributions?"

Marc put down his coffee cup. "It's too early for me to know for sure, but my gut instinct is no."

"You need to figure it out. Like yesterday. The sooner we can determine where this investigation is going the better. We need closure before the election. Not after. Do you understand?"

"Perfectly." Marc had his work cut out for him. The mission had just gotten a lot more complicated. And dangerous.

✳ ✳ ✳

Viv fidgeted as they put on the finishing touches of her makeup. As she predicted, it had taken a bit of work to hide the dark circles under her eyes. She just needed to push through this interview and then there would be time to reassess.

"You're all done, Ms. Reese."

"Thank you." She walked up toward the set where the producer hooked her up with a microphone.

Her interviewer was Steve Scrubbs. A name she was convinced had to be a stage name of sorts. He was quite famous in news circles and known for tough questioning. He smiled at her and then winked. What was this guy up to?

She fielded questions on foreign policy with ease. He'd said at the beginning he'd really like to focus there. Then he took a moment, and she had no idea what was coming.

"Ms. Reese, there's one more topic I'd like to cover today with you."

"All right." Okay here comes the zinger about the Middle East Peace Process or loose nukes.

"Ms. Reese." He paused. "It has come to our attention at CBW news that you are the victim of a stalker. That he even tried to break into your home last night." He leaned in toward her and raised an eyebrow. "Is that the case?"

She sat there shocked. She was in the business of speaking, but right now when she really needed them… no words.

He nodded. "I understand that this must be a difficult topic for you."

She quickly regained her composure. "I'm here to talk about the campaign, Steve. Not about anything else."

"Yes, I understand that. But what if your stalker and the campaign are linked? Do you know if the Senator is under any threat?"

Out of the corner of her eye, she saw Marc making a motion for her to cut Steve off. And she planned to do just that.

"Steve, thank you for the interview and having me on your program today, but I have no further comments." She knew it was highly unorthodox for the campaign spokesperson to basically walk out, but she had no choice. She smiled at the camera and hoped they would cut to save themselves the embarrassment. Then she heard the director cut the shot.

"We're not live anymore."

She pulled the mic off, infuriated that she'd been blindsided. As she started to walk off set, Steve followed and caught up by her side. "Vivian, I'm sorry, but that was a legitimate topic. I can't believe you weren't prepared for it."

She turned to face him directly. "Do you realize that if there was a threat against the Senator how stupid your questions were? I'd have to reveal information about an on-going investigation, which is illegal, not to mention the fact that I would be putting the Senator in danger. And did you think of what your questions would mean for me, personally and for my security? I know your job is to find the story, but sometimes common sense has to prevail. Why didn't you ask me on off the record?"

"I feel that the public has the right to know everything that might involve their future president, and if I alerted you to my final questions I figured you'd give me the run around. And from your response, I can see I was right."

"What the hell is going on here?" Marc's deep voice caught her attention.

"Who is that?" Steve asked her.

"That," she said, "is part of the team's security detail."

"Secret Service?"

"No comment," Marc said.

Viv could tell Marc didn't want to provide this guy with any additional information. He stood with arms crossed and a narrowed brow. He looked like he could snap Steve into pieces.

"We're done here, Steve," she snapped.

"Vivian, this is a tough business. Get used to it." Steve muttered something else under his breath and walked away.

"How did the news of my stalker get out so fast?" she asked Marc.

"You're the PR person, you tell me." He didn't soften his stance.

"Hey, this isn't my fault. I couldn't have known he would ask that."

"I knew this appearance was a bad idea."

She groaned. "I'm not going to stop doing my job because of some psycho, but that leak is disturbing. It had to come from local police or the Secret Service."

Marc's phone rang. "It's Ralph. I guess they were watching back at headquarters." He pushed the talk button. "Yes." He paused while Ralph spoke on the side of the phone. She tapped her foot anxiously, waiting for him to finish the call.

He placed his phone back in his pocket. "We need to return to headquarters, and the Senator wants to speak to you there."

"Great, could this get any worse?" She ran a hand through her hair. "I'm probably about to be fired."

"I don't think that's the case." He grabbed her arm and guided her out of the TV station.

They rode in silence to headquarters, and she was pissed. This was not her doing. Someone had tried to break into her house, and now she was going to be paying for it.

As she walked inside headquarters, she told herself to count to ten and calm down. She was a great crisis manager. She could handle this.

The Senator immediately walked out of his office to meet her. "Let's talk in my office."

Much to her dismay it was her worst fear. Sitting in the Senator's office was Arthur and Abby. This couldn't be good.

"Have a seat, Viv," he said. His expression was grim as he took off his suit jacket.

She sat down and was filled with dread.

The Senator kept talking. "We have a situation on our hands here. I was fully debriefed by Ralph earlier today, and then just now. We all saw what happened on the TV with Steve. You had no prior warning that he was going to ask about that did you?"

"None, sir. I mean, the break in just happened early this morning. The only people that knew about it were local police, Secret Service and Marc. Someone had to have tipped off the press. I don't know why."

Arthur's face had grown animated with widened eyes. He stood up and started pacing. "I'll tell you why. Someone is obviously a friend to the President, and thought that by leaking this story it would hurt our campaign. But they were wrong."

"What do you mean?" she asked.

Arthur put his hands in the air. "Young and beautiful campaign spokeswoman stalked by psycho. I couldn't have written this better myself."

"I'm so confused," Viv said. What was he talking about? "You think it's good that someone tried to break into my house last night?" She heard her voice go up an octave.

"No, of course not. But if it happened, better use it for our benefit."

"Arthur's right," Abby piped in. "This will play in our favor."

The Senator frowned. "I don't care about my campaign if it means one of my people is under attack. This is ridiculous. I know you're my senior staff, but you two have lost your minds."

She could tell he was not happy. He kept talking and looked at her directly. "I want Marc to be by your side every second of the day, do you hear me?"

"Yes, sir," she answered.

"I'll try to talk some sense into my two chief operators here. In the meantime, all campaign security is stepped up per orders from the Secret Service. You should still do your TV spots, but we will have a hard and fast rule, that we will not appear if they want to discuss an active criminal investigation. Is everyone clear about all of this?"

No one said a word. "Viv, you can go. I'd like to talk to these two alone."

She stood up from her chair.

"And, Viv. Be careful, okay?"

"Yes, thank you sir."

She walked out of the room, and was glad she wasn't present for what was going to take place. The Senator rarely got angry, but the glowing look in his eyes told her he was about to dress those two down. She couldn't blame him. Arthur and Abby's jobs were to be political, but under these circumstances, they were being a bit extreme.

When she reached the center of the main room, it got eerily quiet. All eyes were on her. It was clear by now that everyone had heard about what happened. "Don't you all have work to be doing?" she snapped.

The buzz started up again, and she shook her head disgusted by it all. Marc appeared by her side.

"Why don't I take you home? You have to be exhausted."

"That's a great idea."

"Let's tell Ralph that we're out of here."

Ralph's gaze went to them as they started walking, and he met them halfway.

"Sorry about all of this, Viv. I seem to be doing a lot of apologizing lately."

"Do you think it was one of your guys?" she asked.

"Honestly, I don't. My guys aren't political. They're service-oriented, and not a one of them would want to put you in harm's way. My money is on the locals."

"Ugh," she groaned.

"We are moving full speed with our investigation. We put a rush on the prints, and we'll know something later today. I'm also checking all the surveillance footage again from here."

"I'm taking Viv home," Marc said.

"Good idea. I'll keep you posted. Viv, get some rest. Hopefully this will be over soon, and you can return to your normal campaigning."

* * *

He'd been called out on national TV today. In a way it was exhilarating, but they would not like it. The look on Viv's face was of pure horror. It delighted him. He was expecting another call any minute berating him for his stupidity. He'd already received one immediately after the fact. He was ordered to keep a low profile and do some information gathering. Well, he'd obviously gone far beyond that. He had a mission to do. Those men needed to respect him.

When he'd agreed to their terms, he had no idea what his precious Vivian would really be like. Now he had to have her, whatever the cost. He hadn't counted on the hired muscle stepping in so aggressively. How would he get to her? He'd have to be creative.

He was positioned in his normal spot down her street, waiting to make his move. He could wait. It didn't surprise him that she had come home earlier with the muscle, but the muscle would have to leave her at some point. He didn't need long. Even five minutes, and he'd be able to get her. Then what would the muscle do, having failed his only task? He laughed. That would be wondrous. No one would ever suspect him. She'd never see him coming.

His phone buzzed in his pocket, and he cursed when he saw the text but he knew who it was. He had been summoned. He got in his-beat up truck and made the drive to the agreed upon spot.

He hated leaving Viv with the muscle, but for now he had to do their bidding.

He arrived at the meeting place a few minutes late. They'd just have to wait on him. They needed him. Someone with his skills and abilities. He didn't know what all of their larger plans entailed, but he knew someone important was calling the shots. How important, he didn't know. He hated the Senator, so anything he could do to hurt him was fine. But Viv, he needed some special time with. He wouldn't let those other men touch her. She was his. Only his.

"You're late," the gruff familiar voice said.

"I'm a busy man. What do you need?" He saw the gun, but it was too late. He felt the pressure in his chest and the world went dark. His last thought was of his precious Vivian.

***

Viv's entire body ached from pure exhaustion. Marc offered to order pizza and that was perfectly fine with her. She wasn't really in the mood to go anywhere. She'd changed into her sweats and couldn't care less about looking attractive right now. She was having a crappy couple of days and wanted to wallow. Talk about high highs and low lows. She sighed and curled her furry sock-covered feet up under her on the couch. Willow purred loudly next to her.

Marc was talking on his phone to the pizza place. He was ordering enough to feed a small army. Did they really need more than one? He ended the call and sat down beside her on the sofa.

"Sounds like you're hungry."

"You can never have enough pizza." He smiled and then looked directly at her. "Seriously, though. How are you holding up?" He reached out and gently touched her thigh, sending a jolt of heat through her body.

"Glad to be home." She twisted her hair up into a makeshift bun.

"I did not see that Steve guy coming. He was determined to get his story out about your stalker."

She laughed. "Obviously I didn't either. I can't believe Arthur and Abby are ready to spin this thing into something favorable for the campaign. I guess I should think more like them, but I can't."

"And what did the Senator think of their plans?"

"He was pissed. I don't know what he told them after I left the meeting. He rarely lets his emotions show like that."

They watched TV in silence until the doorbell rang signaling the pizza's arrival. Viv could almost taste the cheesy goodness.

"You want to eat in the kitchen or living room?"

"Let's live on the edge and eat in here. I'll go grab some plates and napkins." Viv wanted to keep her butt glued to the comfortable sofa, but she reluctantly gathered supplies from the kitchen. Her stomach rumbled, and she felt like she could eat a whole pizza. Now she was glad about Marc's ordering when she saw two large pizzas sitting on the coffee table. One had extra cheese. The other was piled with every type of meat and not a single veggie. It didn't seem like Marc wasn't going anywhere tonight.

Viv took a bite of the pizza and the flavor of tomato sauce and cheese hit her tongue. She moaned.

"That good, huh?"

She giggled. "Sorry. It is pretty amazing, though."

"Eat up. You need your strength."

While she talked a big game, by the time she'd finished the second slice of extra cheese pizza, she was pretty much stuffed. Marc, on the other hand, had no problem finishing off four slices of the pizza covered in meat.

"Why don't you relax? We can watch a movie," he said. "I'll clean this up." He gathered the pizza boxes and took them to the kitchen.

He returned and sat down beside her on the couch.

"You choose the movie," she said.

"You better be careful, you might not like what I choose."

"Just no horror stories where a woman is stalked and killed."

"That's not even funny, Viv." His dark eyes serious as he watched her.

"I know."

He put on an old school action flick and she cuddled up beside him, resting her head on his shoulder and pulling a blanket around them both.

She became lost in a deep all too familiar nightmare.

***

Marc watched Viv sleep. From what he could tell it wasn't exactly a peaceful slumber. Maybe she'd be more comfortable if he took her up to her bedroom. The bigger question was whether he had the self-control necessary to deliver her to bed and then come back downstairs.

She murmured something that he couldn't understand and twisted into a little ball. That was it. He couldn't stand to see her like that. He carefully scooped her up and hoped he wouldn't wake her. He could tell by how quiet she was at dinner that she was worn out. He couldn't blame her.

He walked into her room and gently placed her down on the bed. Then he couldn't help his natural curiosity, so he took a moment to look around. Who knew that the woman who liked to have a beer at Irish pubs and shoot whiskey would have a softer side? Her room wasn't over the top girly, but he noticed furry pink slippers tucked under the side of the bed leading to the master bath. Also, her bed was covered with a large ivory down comforter and was topped with beige throw pillows. Sophisticated. Just like Viv.

Watching her steady breathing made him want to slide in next to her and wrap his arms around her. But that would only be the start. There was no way he could stop there. He thought about trying to pull the comforter up over her, but he didn't want to disturb her. She actually looked like she was resting comfortably.

It was time for him to go back downstairs while he still could. It didn't stop him from thinking about how much he wanted Viv to invite him into her bedroom and then into her bed. Maybe one day.

He finished watching the movie on his own and was about to walk to the guestroom to get some shut eye when his cell phone rang.

"Hello," he answered.

"Hey, it's Ralph. We've got a big development."

"What happened?" He felt his heart pound in anticipation.

"Viv's stalker. A guy named Oscar Penzer. He's been located."

"Where?"

"That's the thing. It's all a bit crazy. His dead body was found near campaign headquarters. Single gunshot wound. Pictures of Viv were in the backpack that he was wearing. We also discovered that he has priors for assault and solicitation. His prints match the partial we were able recover from the note."

"Wow."

"Let's discuss more in person. I'll be over there soon."

Marc hung up the phone and couldn't believe it. He had a sinking feeling that this wasn't the end of things. But he owed it to Viv to let her know what was happening.

He touched her shoulder gently, but she didn't respond. Then he touched her a little harder, and she bolted upright.

"Sorry, Viv. It's just me, Marc. I've been trying to wake you, but you seemed totally in another world."

"What's wrong?"

"They caught your stalker. A guy named Oscar Penzer, and he has a record—previously arrested for solicitation and assault."

"What? How?"

"His dead body was dumped right down the block from headquarters. Local PD found him."

"How do they know it's him?"

"He had his ID on him. Plus plenty of pictures of you in his bag."

"Oh God."

"Yeah, but at least this looks like this ends it."

"What about the investigation into his murder?"

"It will be investigated by local PD and the Secret Service. It's way too early to determine what happened."

"I don't know what to say."

"You don't have to say anything right now. Go back to sleep. I put you in the bed when you fell asleep watching the movie. I just wanted to let you know as soon as I heard. Maybe you'll sleep better now. I'll just be in the other room if you need me, though."

Marc closed Viv's door and walked down to the living room and waited for Ralph to arrive.

Ralph scowled when Marc opened the door and invited him in.

"Let's talk in the kitchen," Marc said. He'd made some fresh coffee and took a big gulp. "I don't like this one bit. Our stalker gets a bullet through the chest and his body is dumped by campaign headquarters?"

"I agree with you. You didn't say that to Viv did you?" Ralph asked, reaching for his cup of coffee.

"No. I want her to feel better, not worse. So what do you think's going on here?"

"All I've got is theories. Theory number one. This is random. I think we can quickly dismiss that, but had to say it. Theory number two is that our stalker was working with someone that turned on him. That's the more likely scenario. But why? And what were they working together for?"

"Well maybe they didn't like the national TV exposure from the CBW interview."

"What's the end game though?" Ralph asked.

"Some kind of negative impact on the campaign? Maybe Oscar took it too far, and his partner got cold feet? Or maybe the partner is planning something bigger. I'm assuming extra security will still be in place for the Senator?"

"Definitely. And I don't want you to leave Viv yet. Not until we know more both from the crime scene and the larger investigation."

"You got it."

"All right. I'm going to get home. See you tomorrow at headquarters."

CHAPTER FIVE

A week later

"I don't understand why you still have to shadow me. There've been no additional threats to anyone at the campaign including me. The guy is dead. It's over." Viv paced around her office at headquarters, feeling Marc breathe down her neck. She couldn't tamper down the attraction she felt toward him.

"Humor me," Marc said, as he briefly touched her shoulder.

She crossed her arms. "I think you're just trying to get me to go out with you. Or should I say, stay in with you?"

He laughed. "I'm not gonna say I'd turn you down. But believe it or not, sex is not my top priority right now. Your safety is."

She heard a loud roar of voices from the main room with all the TVs. "What the hell is going on?" She jogged from her office with Marc right behind her. She stared at the TV screen, but couldn't hear the commentator for all the noise.

"Be quiet!" she yelled. No one stopped talking.

Marc put his hands up to his mouth and whistled. The room went silent.

"What happened on the news?" she asked the group of campaign workers stand around.

One young staffer piped up. "The President's campaign headquarters in DC were vandalized."

What? She pushed through the crowd so she could read the TV screen. Scrolling in big letters on CBW was just that story.

She turned and looked for Marc who given the look on his face was already in a deep conversation with Ralph who stood beside him. She listened for a moment to Steve Scrubbs detail the story. Someone spray painted all over the headquarters and busted out a side window. There was video footage, but the Secret Service had yet to provide any comment about what the tape showed.

Viv walked over to Marc and Ralph.

"Viv, I need you to stay here," Marc said softly. "I'm going with Ralph to assist his team for a bit."

"Where else would I go? This is where I work." She tensed her fingers. They clearly were trying to keep her in the dark again. But she needed to get her head in the game and think about how this story would play out in the press. And she intended to do just that.

"I'll be back," Marc said.

"Great," she said, but they had already started walking away.

$$* * *$$

Marc's thoughts were going in a million different directions. Ralph had only told him that they needed to talk at his office at Secret Service headquarters. Marc knew something serious was going on. Was his cover blown? Or was this another issue entirely? He had to keep it together until he knew exactly what he was dealing with.

They arrived at Ralph's office, and Marc couldn't keep quiet any longer.

"So what is happening here?" He stood facing Ralph.

Ralph pursed his lips. "I brought you here because I need to show you something."

"All right. What is it?"

"Better for me to just roll the tape." Ralph motioned for him to take a look at the TV screen. "This is from last night when the President's campaign headquarters was vandalized."

Marc watched the screen intently focused on the images. "Shit," he muttered. On the screen, an image appeared outside the campaign office that looked eerily like Viv.

"You can say that again," Ralph said. "What I need you to tell me is how this is even possible? You were supposed to be on Viv all the time."

"I don't know. This makes no sense. I was with her." Marc started pacing back and forth.

"Look at the time stamp. Two a.m."

"We were at her house."

"So she snuck out."

"That couldn't have happened."

"Why is that?"

"I would've known, dammit." There had to be some other explanation.

"I can see the doubt all over your face." Ralph took a step closer to him.

"No. I can tell you right now. No way in hell she could've gotten past me. It has to be someone else. There is no doubt. Only confusion."

"Man, I'm with you. I don't want it to be her either. But look. The height fits. She's a small woman." Ralph pointed to the screen. "The floodlights show her dark hair in that ponytail under her hat. And it's a Georgetown hat."

"If she was going to be so stupid, and I say if, she'd never wear a Georgetown hat."

"It could've been impulse. All the stress with the stalker and the murder, in addition to the campaign. It caught up with her and she snapped." Ralph made a motion with his hands.

"I'm telling you, she did not leave the condo last night. Something smells fishy here."

"It does, but all the evidence points to her. We're going to have to question her."

"Why question her? If you really suspected her, wouldn't you stay on her? Figure out what she's up to?" Marc sunk down in the chair in Ralph's office and rubbed his now aching temples. He had to determine what had really happened.

"We can't take a risk like that. This isn't war games. This is the President we're talking about here. Hopefully, this was just bad judgment, but I don't take chances like this."

"I understand your role here. All I can tell you is she isn't the person in that video."

"What do you remember about last night?" Ralph walked behind his desk and took a seat.

"Sounds like I'm the one being interviewed now."

"It's easier if we just get this over with."

"Okay. We got home from the office about twenty-one hundred."

"Enough with the military speak. Eight p.m. I get it."

"We ordered Chinese food. I had a little scotch. I was in bed by midnight. Didn't wake up until five thirty. Slept through the night."

"Is it unusual for you to sleep through?"

Marc looked down and knew with each word out of his mouth, he was digging the hole against Viv deeper and deeper. "A little but not unheard of. And before you ask, no I didn't drink that much."

"I'd like you to have a blood test done right now. See if we can find anything in your system."

Marc raised his eyebrow. "You really think she dosed me?"

Ralph shrugged. "No crazier than her breaking a window at the President's campaign headquarters."

"That's only true if you're right about her." Marc shook his head, disgusted. Yeah, he'd wanted to figure out her role in his own investigation, but this was on a different level. Viv was innocent in this mess.

"I'll take you down to medical for your blood test. Then someone will bring you back here, and we can figure out the next move."

"Fine." Marc was escorted by Ralph to medical, but he was able to get a minute alone in the bathroom that he used to make a call to Peter. He knew his tests would come back clean.

"Peter, we've got a situation." Marc relayed everything he knew to Peter. "Do I out myself to the Secret Service?"

"No, no. Not yet. Our investigation still needs to function. Let the Secret Service do their jobs, and you keep doing yours. They can run parallel. We need complete independence to keep our investigation from becoming tainted."

"I hear that, sir."

"You understand?"

"Yes, sir."

"Obviously don't obstruct their investigation. Who knows where this whole thing is going to go, but you need to remember there's still a possibility of illegal contributions in the Nelson campaign. It's our job to be on top of that."

"Understood."

Marc finished his call and the blood work and was taken back to Ralph's office.

"So what next?"

"I've made some calls. The higher ups actually agreed with the strategy that we need you to stick to her. If you want my opinion, I think the political crowd poked their noses in. They're worried about what will happen if the Secret Service starts questioning the rival campaign's spokeswoman. A woman who was targeted by a stalker and is currently a media darling."

"But you're the one focused on the tape."

"Yeah, I still think it's her." Ralph cocked his head to the side. "But anything can be faked. We need more evidence to build a case. For her sake, I hope this was a one-time indiscretion."

"I still don't think she's involved, but either way this is not good."

"I know. I also understand you were hired by the campaign, but you've signed a cooperation agreement with us. You could legally bail, but if you're going to do that, I ask you do it now, before things get even more complicated."

"No." Marc shook his head. "I'm not quitting. I'm in."

"So the plan is for you to stay on her. We can say that given what happened to the President's office, and the unresolved murder of the stalker, she needs the special level of security. And fix your own drinks. Who knows what she has up her sleeves."

"You really think she's into something here?"

"I don't know. But all my instincts are telling me something is really wrong. I'm just trying to piece it together. I know you think she's not capable of this, but I'm asking you to just do the job you're assigned."

Marc nodded. "Roger that." He did intend to stick by Viv. But his mission was to protect her. His gut screamed at him. She was in grave danger.

***

Viv was trying to focus on responding to media inquiries regarding the vandalism. Of course, she didn't condone the vandalism, but it was getting old having to repeat the same line over and over again. She didn't want to be cute and get caught in a snafu saying something that would make the Senator or his campaign look callous. They also had to be careful not to appear like political opportunists. So much thought and strategy had to go into every word she said. It was tiring, and her head started to pound.

"I'm back."

She turned and looked at Marc. "What was all that cloak and dagger stuff with Ralph?"

"Our friends at the Secret Service get really nervous when stuff like this happens. But they've got their act together. The President's own detail is adding extra security, and Ralph will be in charge of any changes here and making sure the Nelson campaign is safe."

"Where does that leave me?" she asked knowing she probably wasn't going to like the answer.

"You're still stuck with me. This latest incident means there may be a broader security threat involving both campaigns. The murder of the stalker is still not resolved. We've got a lot more questions than answers. It's for your own safety, and the Senator has already approved it. He's really worried about you. He's still shaken from the break in at your condo. I think he feels responsible."

"That's silly. Of course it's not his fault."

"That's the rational response, but it's clear he cares about you. It'd be on his conscious if something happened to you while working for his campaign and supporting him day in and day out. No one feels comfortable with the unresolved murder of your stalker. And now with this vandalism, the assessment is that everyone needs to be on higher alert."

"I was beginning to think you weren't coming back."

"Sorry, it's late. Once you get in the bureaucratic maze, it's hard as hell to come out on the other side unscathed much less quickly. I did the best I could." He gave her a goofy smile, and her stomach flipped.

She could say she didn't want him around, but that would be a total lie. She'd enjoyed spending time with him and their nightly chats over dinner. The funny thing was he hadn't tried to make another move on her since he originally kissed her. It kinda hurt her ego. Maybe she'd fallen squarely into the dreaded friend zone. That's the last place she wanted to be with him. But she needed to be there. For her own sanity and to keep the promise to herself. No alpha males. She couldn't start depending on him. Not now.

"Just give me a minute to wrap up, and we can go."

He nodded and walked away.

She had time to make a quick call to Serena who picked up on the second ring.

"God, Viv. Have you been watching the news?"

"Yes. You're okay, right? I know you don't usually work at the campaign office."

"Yeah, I'm fine, but it's insane. First your stalker. Now this. Maybe there's just some crazy anarchist group out there targeting both campaigns. Or something."

"I know." She tapped her fingers nervously on her desk.

"You still have your extra security you told me about?"

"Yes. That's one of the reasons I called."

"Is everything okay with him?"

"Yes and no. Serena," she lowered her voice to a whisper, "I think I've—um—acquired a bit of a crush on my bodyguard. This is kind of ridiculous, but in all honesty I've really got the hots for him. I know I shouldn't make a move, but…"

She was met with silence for a few seconds. "Viv, there's nothing wrong with making a move. As long as you see it for what it is. This wouldn't be a relationship. You said he's hot. Well, enjoy him. You deserve some no strings attached fun. Especially after all you've been through over the past couple weeks. First with Gene getting sick, the new job, and the stalker. So give yourself a break. Not everything in life has to be so serious."

"I hear you, but I'm afraid I'm not going to be nearly as good at this as you are. How do you do it?"

Serena laughed. "You mean screw around like a man? It takes practice. But once you get the hang of it, you'll never be lonely again."

Viv couldn't help but laugh too. She didn't know what she'd do without Serena.

"Seriously, Viv. At least give yourself one night. If you can't hang, then cut it off."

"You're a great friend, Rena."

"Thanks. Hey, I've gotta run, things are still crazy around here. But call me again soon, okay?"

"Yeah. Be careful." She hung up and knew what she had to do tonight.

* * *

Viv had almost talked herself out of it by the time they reached her condo. They'd stopped at the Thai place Marc had introduced her to and grabbed a quick dinner. As she lounged in the living room on her couch, she ran through all types of scenarios in her head. There was something about that sparkle in his chocolate eyes that she couldn't turn away from. But what if he rejected her? Wouldn't that sting? She'd faced rejection before. But, that was more rejection from a relationship, not sex. This was sex. Serena's words pounded in her head. She could do this. It would be liberating, right? She was going to have no strings attached sex and enjoy it. She leaned her head back on the couch for a moment and then lifted it back up.

"What's on your mind?" Marc asked.

"Everything," she said, trying to avoid the real topic.

"You need to relax." He walked into her kitchen and came back into the living room with two glasses of whiskey. He was getting to know her too well. He'd made himself at home since he'd been staying there so much and sleeping in her guestroom. Now she wanted him in her bed.

"Thanks. I haven't been sleeping well. I think I'm just tired."

It occurred to her that she had absolutely no idea what she was going to do. Guys usually made the first move. She couldn't remember a time when she initiated anything physical with a guy.

Now, looking at Marc, she couldn't figure him out. He'd been the aggressor at the beginning, but lately he'd been completely hands off. Should she just try something or talk about it? God, she was so bad at this. She took a sip of the whiskey and hoped that would give her some courage to actually go after what she wanted. And she wanted him.

"Hey," he said. "Come here."

She scooted closer to him, and he started his now familiar shoulder massage. He had no problem doing this, but he never attempted to take it any further. He would simply finish the massage and move away.

She couldn't stand it any longer. His large hands felt so warm and strong on her body. She wanted more. She needed more. She turned around to face him on the couch. His hands were still on her shoulders. It was now or never. She leaned and brushed her lips against his. He seemed tentative for about two seconds. And then. Fireworks.

"Viv," he murmured. His hands were everywhere. Rubbing down her back, around and back up her sides. His lips were hungry and as he opened his mouth she felt his tongue tangle with her own. She didn't have a chance to back out now. This was happening.

He pulled her onto his lap so she was straddling his large muscular thighs. His body felt even better against hers than she'd imagined. She started tugging at his shirt, and he did the same. When he removed her top and found her purple lace bra he cursed. "Damn, Viv. You are gorgeous."

He kissed down her neck and then started kissing her breast through her bra. She literally felt like she was going to explode right there. Had it been that long? It felt like it had been an eternity, and nothing she'd ever experienced was this steamy. This was her decision. She was in control. There was something about Marc, and the way he said her name, the way he touched her, that she couldn't resist.

She ran her hand down his chest and felt his hard abs. Chiseled to perfection. He nibbled her ear, and she started grinding her body against him. This was something she wanted, she reminded herself.

"I have a better idea," he whispered, his voice ragged.

She couldn't form words, so she just nodded. He picked her up from the sofa as if she weighed nothing and carried her into the bedroom. She'd wished she'd had one more drink to give her that final boost of courage. He must have sensed her reluctance once they got into the bedroom, and he gently placed her down on the bed.

"Viv, we can stop. I know that things ramped up quickly. I just couldn't help myself." His dark eyes were even darker than usual as he took hurried breaths. Was she really doing that to this man? It made her want him even more. He was giving her a graceful out. If she was going to bail, now was the time.

"Viv, look at me."

She looked up at him, and knew what she wanted. She said nothing as she laid down and pulled him in for another kiss. This was it. She was going for it. Just like Serena had coached her. She started fumbling around with his zipper.

"Here, let me." He quickly removed his shoes and pants and was back with her on the bed. He started kissing her again and licked through her bra. Then he lifted her up slightly and removed it completely. For a moment, he just looked at her. So much so that she was afraid she had done something wrong.

"What?" she asked.

"I'm speechless. You're amazing, Viv. Honestly, I'd fantasized about what it would be like to see your body, but this is so much better than my fantasy."

Hearing his compliments gave her a needed boost of self-confidence. She ran her hands down his broad muscular back to his ass. He wore fitted boxed briefs, and she could feel the hardness of him in between her legs.

She sighed as he continued to kiss down her body. He skill-fully removed her pants and her underwear. Then he kissed up her thighs and by the time he reached her center she was on fire. It only took a few flicks of his tongue before her first orgasm hit her. She was almost ashamed that she had been affected that quickly. But when she looked up and saw the grin on his face, that all faded away.

He kissed her again and removed his boxers.

"Wait," she said, grabbing at his shoulders. "Do you have protection?"

"Yes, ma'am." He reached down to the floor for his pants and pulled out a condom. Quickly he put it on and his lips were back on her skin tasting her body. He was so strong he was able to allow part of his weight to fall on her while holding the rest of his body up.

He nudged her legs apart and started to enter her. She expected him to be fast about it. But he wasn't. He was gentle. Nudging deeper and deeper until her body fully accepted him.

She sighed. He felt wonderful inside of her. He started to move, and she moved with him. Everything about this was per-fect, unlike anything she'd ever experienced before. As he entered her more deeply, she felt a second wave of pleasure wash over her, engulfing all her muscles down to her toes.

"I want to see you," he said. He rolled them over, and she was on top. She felt a bit self-conscious, but the desire on his face let her know he wanted her. His eyes were glued to hers, but she closed her eyes after a minute and just enjoyed the moment. Then grinding on top of him she could feel him tighten under her, and he called out her name. She felt one more blast of pleasure and collapsed on top of him. It was the most amazing feeling of her life.

What had she just done?

***

Marc couldn't see her face as the room was very dark, but he didn't have to. He could tell she was already starting to second-guess her decision. He couldn't blame her. Rationally thinking they should not have just done what they just did. But their reasons for regret were extremely different. Yeah, he'd been encouraged to get closer to her via any means necessary, but that isn't what just happened. The last thing on his mind had been his investigation. He wanted her. And she wanted him. But now things were going to get complicated. He couldn't reveal his true purpose for joining the Nelson campaign and to make matters worse, she was now on the Secret Service's radar because of that stupid tape.

The woman he was holding in his arms would not have done that. Yeah, he hadn't known her that long, but he trusted his instincts. Always had and always would. His instincts were screaming at him that he needed to get closer to Viv to protect her. Not to treat her as a suspect.

Regardless, he still had work to do, and he wasn't going to forget his initial mission. But he also needed to keep Viv safe, not just for the campaign, but also for his own sanity. Completing both and coming out on the other end unscathed, was going to be a difficult. But he couldn't afford to fail. He would be lying to himself if he tried to say that Viv was just another woman. There was something different about her. She was the last thing he thought he wanted and everything he needed. How could he be into a woman whose entire life was politics?

Viv let out a little sigh, but he didn't think it was time to talk. He kept his arms wrapped tightly around her, and she didn't try to move. He took that as a good sign. His thoughts went back to that surveillance video. Could someone have doctored the tape? Of course. But they'd have to be good, or have a stand in that looked eerily like Viv. Given the grainy nature of the surveillance footage that was possible. He was determined to find out who it was to clear Viv's name.

Ralph was going to kill him when he found out that Marc was FBI, but it wasn't really Marc's problem. He was just following orders, and Ralph would have to accept that. Peter had been very clear that he was to keep his cover intact. No deviations. So that's exactly what he planned to do.

CHAPTER SIX

iv was relieved when Serena was able to meet for coffee. Marc had agreed to drop her off at the coffee shop and leave her unattended, as he called it, as long as she promised not to leave until he got back to escort her.

He'd been acting strange that morning. Not distant, actually affectionate. A different side to him, really. But there was something brewing beneath the surface that she couldn't quite put her finger on. She knew sex would change things, but she wondered if something else was also going on with him. They hadn't talked about what had happened at all.

She walked into the coffee shop, and the wonderful aromas awoke all her senses. Coffee was a major weakness for her. She didn't need all the fancy sugary drinks—just coffee. As usual, Serena was late. She'd gotten used to her best friend's time schedule long ago. It didn't bother Viv. She decided to splurge on a scone and ordered her coffee. Taking the warm mug in her hand, she found a table for the two of them.

After a few minutes, Serena bounded into the coffee shop. Her long black hair was pulled back in a low ponytail, and she wore a perfectly tailored navy suit which fit her tall and slim frame perfectly. She'd paired her suit with a bright purple cami that looked great against her dark skin. Serena was a total knock out.

"Hi there." Viv stood up and hugged her friend tightly.

"I'm sorry I've been so out of the loop. Things have been crazy, and now with this vandalism, everyone is up in arms." Serena fussed with her ponytail and then unbuttoned her suit jacket.

"Yeah, it's crazy at our headquarters too."

Serena leaned back in her chair and then popped forward in her seat. "Oh my God. You had sex with him last night, didn't you?"

Viv looked down and felt her cheeks flush. "Uh, why do you ask?"

"You look refreshed and glowing. I am so proud of you!"

Viv smiled. "You gave good advice. I tried to follow it."

"I want to hear all about it, but let me get a drink first."

Viv tried to give herself a pep talk while Serena went up to the bar and ordered.

Serena walked back to the table carrying her usual latte. "Spill it."

Viv sighed and took a sip of coffee, enjoying the deep flavors. "It was amazing. Best. Sex. Ever."

Serena gave her a high five. "That's awesome, Viv."

Viv shook her head. "Let's not get ahead of ourselves. Even though it was amazing, I still second guessed myself immediately after."

"Don't do that," she warned sternly. Serena patted Viv's hand. "It will get easier. This is a huge first step."

"I don't know. How do you keep your feelings out of it?"

"By seeing it for what it is. You can't get into bed with expectations of a committed relationship. If you do, they'll get dashed. Unless of course you've found the perfect man, and those qualifications are: hot in bed, smart, funny, and not a cheater. I'm convinced that's about point one percent of the male population. Only those men deserve to be relationship material. Until you find that, have some fun. You work far too hard not to enjoy yourself."

"Thanks for giving me some perspective. I'm not going to pretend like this is easy. The 'what ifs' popped into my mind as soon as it was over. And then the, 'what have I done,' followed right after that."

"Viv, look at me. There's nothing wrong with the fact that you enjoyed having sex with the guy. I realize we don't ever really talk about it much, but I know that you being forced to grow up so quickly when your parents died makes you value your independence even more. And that's perfectly understandable. What I'm suggesting is that this process can and should be something to make you feel independent and in control."

"I guess I just lack confidence after the whole cheating fiasco with Scott. I don't know that I can trust my instincts like I thought I could. So it makes me wary."

"I know I'm giving you all this advice, but that's short term, Viv. Just remember you're going to find a man one day who loves you and respects you. And you're going to love him in the same way."

Viv had talked enough about her emotional baggage for one day. "How about you? What's going on with your man?"

Serena leaned in closer. "If I tell you, Viv, you have to swear not to tell anyone."

"You know you can trust me."

"I know I can, but this is even a little crazy for me."

"Oh, no. Rena, what have you done?"

Serena blushed a little and diverted her eyes. This was an unusual side to her, and Viv knew that she was in something deep. Serena never got embarrassed by anything. And especially not around Viv.

"Start at the beginning. I know there's a guy you've been hanging out with. Tell me more."

"He's amazing." She sighed. "There's only one catch."

"Don't tell me you're dating a married man, Rena."

"No. Even I have some morals," she said, as she held her head up high.

"Okay, then how bad could it be?"

Serena took a deep breath and leaned in close. "He's a Secret Service agent."

Viv grimaced. "And since you're a member of the President's staff, he should be completely off limits."

"Exactly." Serena leaned back. "But, Viv, he's amazing. Besides being gorgeous, he's so funny and smart."

Viv watched as Serena gushed. And it hit her. Serena had broken her own rules and fallen hard for this guy. "You really like him."

"Yes. I know it's not my usual MO. But he's different."

"He's the one tenth of one percent?"

Serena nodded. "He might be the one."

"Really?" Viv couldn't believe this.

"Yes."

"That's huge." Viv was happy to see the joy in Serena's eyes.

"I'm thinking of resigning."

"What?" Viv sat shocked. Serena loved her job on the White House Staff. It was everything to her and a position at that level was almost impossible to obtain. Their love for politics and policy making was one of the core things the two of them had in common.

"I could still work for the campaign, but I'd need to resign my Staffer position at the White House to prevent the conflict of interest."

"Isn't that drastic?"

Serena nodded. "It is. But I've fallen for this guy."

Viv hated to put a damper on things, but she had to ask. "Are you sure he's all in? How long have you been seeing him?" Viv was a little hurt that Serena would have been keeping this from her.

Serena looked away sheepishly. "It's only been two months."

"Two months?" She heard herself get louder. "You can't quit your Staffer job because of a two month relationship. Serena, this isn't like you at all." Viv wondered what this guy had done to her best friend. The woman she knew would never have given up her job for a man.

"I thought you would be happy for me, Viv." Serena's eyes darkened.

"Oh, I am happy. Very happy. It's just so sudden." She paused to gather her thoughts. "And I don't want you to make any quick decisions that you'll regret. Just promise me you'll give it a little more thought. And if you decide to do it, I will support you a hundred percent."

Viv watched as tears brimmed in Serena's eyes. She worried that something was wrong. She'd only seen Serena cry once in the ten years they'd known each other.

Serena wiped away a tear and grabbed Viv's hand. "Thanks, Viv. I'm lucky to have you in my life."

"And I want to meet this guy."

"You will. I promise. And I want to meet your hunk too."

"You'll get your wish. He's coming to pick me up. Everything has been hectic with security after the stalker stuff. And now with the vandalism against the President's headquarters, Marc is as constant as my shadow."

Serena raised an eyebrow. "Doesn't sound like that's such a bad gig though, right?"

"I like my space. But no, you're right. At first, I was glad he was around. It was all very frightening. Now though, I can't help but feel like he knows something he's not telling me. No one wants me to be alone."

"They're probably just being cautious. The Senator loves you so much. He probably gave that order, and they're just following it."

Viv nodded. "Yeah, I guess you're right." Viv thought back to how upset the Senator was when Arthur and Abby wanted to capitalize on her stalker.

"And as far as your media presence, you've been getting rave reviews all around. I know you realize this, but our people hate you now." Serena laughed. "I'll just leave it at that."

The two women knew that given their respective jobs on the opposite side of the political aisle, they usually couldn't get into deep political conversations. "Thanks."

"Seriously. You're doing a great job. As your best friend, I'm super proud of you, even if as the opponent, I can't stand you." Serena's eyes looked toward the door. "Uh, Viv. There is a huge hot looking hunk staring at you. Wow. I'm assuming that's your bodyguard?"

Viv looked over, and Marc was walking toward them.

He smiled and reached out his hand to Serena. "I'm Marc Locke."

"Serena Hernandez, enemy number one. Pleasure to meet you."

Marc raised his eyebrow. Viv chimed in. "Serena is on the White House Staff."

"Ah," he said. "That's nice that you two can be friends. I can imagine that makes for lively discussions."

Serena laughed. "We usually talk about sex and shoes instead of politics."

Viv thought she was going to die of embarrassment, but Marc just laughed. "Glad to hear it. I'm not into politics, myself."

"But you're into security?" Serena asked.

"Yes, ma'am. I stay above the fray."

"Great. There are plenty of hacks like me and Viv to do all of the dirty work." Serena smiled. "And speaking of work, I should get back. Viv, I'll talk to you later. It was great meeting you, Marc."

"You too," he said. He sat down in Serena's seat. He looked at Viv. "That's crazy that the two of you are friends."

"Not just friends, best friends. We met right after college graduation when we interned on the Hill."

"And your political differences didn't stop you from becoming friends to begin with?"

"No. It was never like that with Serena. Yeah, we support different political parties, but we have more in common than we do differences."

"That's nice to see. Good friends are hard to come by." He paused. "You ready to head out?"

"Sure." She wondered what he meant by the friend comment. Did he have a best friend? It occurred to her there was a lot that she didn't know about Marc.

They were walking to the door, and he leaned down. "I hope I got a shout out in between the sex and shoes talk."

She laughed as he put his hand in the small of her back her guiding her out the door.

***

The next day Marc walked out of Viv's office at campaign headquarters and found Ralph hanging out in the opposite corner of the building.

"What's the latest?" Marc asked.

Ralph leaned against a vacant desk. "The video is inconclusive. We sent the footage to our FBI liaison, and they're determining if it's been digitally altered. We're also working up a list of people on both campaign staffs that fit the description of the lady on the tape."

"You don't think it's her now do you?"

"Man, I've watched that tape a million times, and there's something off." Ralph ran his hand through his hair. "Yeah the features look like her, but the movement doesn't. Maybe I just don't want to believe that it's her."

"I hear you."

"Is there something going on between the two of you?"

"Why do you ask?"

"Because there seems to be a weird undercurrent between the two of you."

"No," he lied. He was in so deep, why not keep digging?

"All right. I just need to know that you can be objective." Ralph crossed his arms.

"You won't have to worry about that."

"Everything is quiet at the President's campaign headquarters. No one has reported anything else. When is Viv going on TV again?"

"I haven't even asked her. I guess I should."

"Have you left her alone at all?"

"She met her friend at a coffee shop yesterday, but I wasn't far. Just gave them a little space." He'd had his eyes on the coffee shop the entire time.

"You notice anything out of the ordinary?"

"Negative."

"I just hope this all blows over. I checked with local PD this morning. No leads on Oscar's murder, which is extremely odd. I hate this uncertainty." He cracked his knuckles.

"Let me get back to Viv and see what her schedule is. I'll keep you posted."

"Thanks."

Ralph seemed antsy, and Marc was frustrated. His investigation was going nowhere fast. Peter wasn't going to be happy with his continued lack of progress. What could he do to speed things along? Maybe he needed to push harder on Viv. He had worried that too many questions would raise suspicions, but given all that was going on, he might have more wiggle room.

He walked into her office and found her typing quickly with her eyes focused on the screen. He took a seat and waited for her to acknowledge him.

After a few minutes, she looked away from the computer. "Yes?"

"When is your next appearance?"

"Tomorrow. Doing the leg-work now to set up other interviews. I also have a VIP I have to talk with."

"What kind of VIP?"

"The kind with deep pockets." She laughed. "Isn't it always about the money?" She started typing. "Do you need anything else?"

She seemed particularly cool. Too cool. Already pulling away. He needed to stop this before she ran away from him.

He closed her door and walked over to where she sat behind the desk. "I can think of a lot of other things I need from you."

Her eyes widened and she opened her mouth to speak, but he crushed his lips hungrily against hers silencing any protest. He could feel her tensing up, but he deepened the kiss further, daring her to stop him. Not allowing her any room to escape. He felt her surrender as she ran her hands through his hair. "Does your door lock?" he asked.

She nodded, and he went back to the door and flipped the lock. He grabbed her up out of her seat and into his arms. He hadn't planned on walking into her office and mauling her, but now it seemed like the best idea he'd ever had in his entire life.

"We shouldn't be doing this," she whispered.

"Don't think," he said. He was surprised she hadn't slammed on the brakes. He kissed her again and started unbuttoning her blouse.

"No," she croaked.

And his hands stopped. He pulled back slightly to look into her eyes. "Hey, when you say no, I'm listening."

She raised an eyebrow. "Thank you."

"You all right?" he asked pulling further away.

"Yes, I just think this isn't such a great idea."

He smiled. "I can wait until we get back to your place."

"No. That's not what I meant. I… uh, mean, in general."

"And what would be your reason for that decision because none are coming to mind at the moment?"

She looked down, seemingly trying to fish up some excuse. "I thought it was just a one-time thing, okay? Can't we just leave it at that? I know you don't want a relationship with me. It was supposed to be fun, you know?"

"Ouch," he said. "I didn't realize I was just a one-time thing. That certainly wasn't what I had in mind. I was hoping… well I guess it doesn't matter what I was hoping. Right?"

"I'm sorry. I didn't mean it like that."

"Yes, apparently you did. I get it. You wanted fun, and I was there to provide it. That's fine with me, babe." He was clearly going to have to re-evaluate his approach. The scowl on her face let him know he'd pissed her off by calling her babe. But hell, she'd been the one to imply he was just a play thing. What a cluster. This wasn't the best idea after all, but he kept thinking about their night together. He needed to shift his focus.

"Wait," she said. She reached out and grabbed his arm.

"No. I think we're done here." He walked out and didn't look back. He needed to regroup.

***

Oh my God. She'd almost had sex with him in her office. She'd really lost it. What was she thinking? She knew she couldn't pull this off. The worst part was that she was actually disappointed when he had backed away from her. And that made her upset at herself. He'd done exactly as she asked. So why was she so mad?

She shouldn't be feeling this strongly for him. It was exactly what she was trying to avoid. She might have said it would be a one-time thing, but there was no way she believed it.

She sighed and pushed a stray hair behind her ear. Get it together. The last thing she needed to be worried about now was a man. She had her dream job, and it was the middle of a hard-fought presidential campaign. The first debate was this week. She should be thrilled, not worried about some stupid guy—regardless of how hot he was. Or how great he made her feel.

CHAPTER SEVEN

Viv was glad she'd decided to take the afternoon off and go shopping. After grabbing a quick bite to eat in the food court, she strolled through the mall. She'd had an internal debate with herself. A debate that led her to walk to the fancy lingerie store.

As she stood outside the store, a prickle of awareness washed over her. Looking around, she saw the same man who had sat at a nearby table where she had eaten lunch just a few minutes ago. Was it just her imagination, or had he followed her? She made eye contact with him, and he looked at her like he knew her. Maybe he just recognized her from seeing her on TV? Maybe she was paranoid after the stalker drama? She glanced over at his direction and noticed that he'd moved away to look at another store window. She needed to stop being silly.

Taking a deep breath, she focused on the next challenge. The lingerie. Why was she even going into the store? Because she clearly didn't want Marc to be a one-time thing. She didn't even want him to be a two-time thing. Putting a number on it didn't seem right. Yeah, she'd told Serena she wanted a fling, but now it was clear to her, she wanted something else, something more.

She walked through the store and was overwhelmed by all the options. Not wanting to go with something too crazy, she settled on a lacy red number that was sexy without being a novelty item. As she stood at the register paying, she sucked in a breath.

The man was standing outside the store. He wasn't looking in her direction, but what if he was waiting on her?

She needed to get a grip. He was probably some poor guy stuck at the mall with his wife or girlfriend trying to pass the time. And if he wasn't? No. She couldn't think that way. She refused to live her life in fear. She paid the cashier and took her shiny pink bag. She'd just walk right out of the store and not give him a second thought.

As she exited the store, she walked straight into him.

"Excuse me," he said, as he reached out and touched her elbow. "Do I know you?"

She looked into his hazel eyes. Not knowing what was going on, she took a step backward. "No, I don't think so."

"You look so familiar. Are you sure we haven't met before?"

"Listen, I don't know who you are. But I suggest you leave me alone, or I'll have to alert the mall security." She really wasn't sure what she'd tell them, but this guy gave her the creeps. He was invading her personal space. She took one more step back.

"I'm sorry. There's no need to get upset. I must be mistaken." He grinned and moved away from her. "Have a good day."

A chill went down her back. Was he just trying to come on to her? She didn't know. Regardless she was ready to walk the other direction.

After a couple of hours, she'd finally worn herself out. She loved the two new suits she carried in her shopping bag along with some great new accessories including two sparkly fun bracelets that were totally impractical. She wondered if she was stupid for buying the lingerie. It could already be over, before it ever really got started. Marc wasn't going to make another move on her. Not after the way she'd treated him. Who could blame him? But there was a small piece of her that was foolishly holding out hope that he would. In that fantasy, she'd have on her new lacy red baby doll.

Her phone buzzed, and she saw Marc was calling.

"Where are you?" he asked, his voice gruff.

"Walking out of the mall. What's going on?"

"You just left and didn't tell me?"

"Uh, yeah. There's no reason for you to be my babysitter. I wanted to go shopping."

He cursed and mumbled something in a low voice that she couldn't make out.

"Marc? What's going on? Are you okay?"

"There's been another incident."

"What type of incident?"

"Let me come get you, and I'll explain."

"But I have my car here. That's silly. I'm on my way home. Just meet me there if you want to talk."

"All right. But go straight home, okay?"

"Marc, you're starting to freak me out. What's going on?"

"I'll explain everything when I get to your condo."

He ended the call, and she was perplexed. She started her car and turned the news to the satellite radio. She didn't hear anything out of the ordinary which meant the news hadn't picked up on whatever Marc was talking about yet.

When she got home, she saw he'd beaten her there. His truck was parked out front. She tucked her tiny lingerie bag into the bigger shopping bag, and walked up to her front door. How had he gotten in? She found him sitting on the sofa giving her a hard look with narrowed eyes.

"How did you get in?" she asked.

"I snagged your spare key from the kitchen pantry the other day. You know, just in case of emergencies."

"And this is an emergency?"

He shrugged noncommittally.

"What's going on?"

"I could ask you the same thing. I thought we'd discussed the fact that I need to provide you protection."

"I wanted to go shopping." She held up her bags. "Somehow I don't see you as wanting to tag alone for that trip."

"Where did you go?"

"The mall. What's wrong? You're starting to worry me."

He sighed and ran his hand through his hair. "The President's war room at the hotel they were working from got ransacked while the advance team was at the debate site."

"Was anyone hurt?"

"No," he said.

"This is all connected isn't it?"

"Viv, we've got an even bigger problem here. There's a reason I asked you not to go anywhere without me. Was anyone with you at the mall?"

She shook her head. "No. But there was a creepy guy who I thought might be following me. I noticed him when I was eating lunch. Then he showed up where I was shopping and asked if we knew each other. I told him to back off."

"Would you be able to describe him to a sketch artist?"

She paused and her heart raced. "I think so."

"Ralph is on his way here to talk to you."

"Why do I feel like I'm missing something? I just went to the mall. I have the receipts." She dug in her purse and showed him the receipts for the two suits and handbag. She wasn't about to show him the lingerie receipt. Now was not the time for total embarrassment.

"So you bought all these between three and four."

"Yes. What's the problem with that?"

"Where were you from noon to three?"

"I left headquarters around one. Went to the mall and had lunch at the food court. Then I did some shopping. But honestly I wasn't keeping a detailed timeline of my activities." She felt her voice shake.

He inched closer to her. "Viv, just calm down a minute. It's going to be okay. We'll get this sorted out."

"There's something you're not telling me."

"Viv, it's not like that, okay?"

"Then tell me what it is like."

He averted his eyes and then made eye contact.

"There's surveillance footage of the person who vandalized the President's headquarters."

"That's good news, right? They can find him."

"Not him. Her."

She was very confused. Why was he telling her this now? "What does this have to do with anything?"

"The person on the tape looked just like you. Georgetown hat and all."

Her stomach dropped. This was not happening. Someone was framing her. It hit her very quickly. "Marc, I didn't do that. You have to believe me. You've been with me for the past two weeks. I'm the victim here."

"I know, Viv. I do. We'll figure out how to clear your name."

Viv felt like her world was crashing down. This would be horrible for the campaign not to mention her personal safety. She felt irrational and slightly out of control. "Do I need to remind you that a man was stalking me? That he tried to break into my house? That he was killed? Shot? Murdered?" After she said it she saw the expression on his face darken. "I certainty did not vandalize the President's headquarters, and all I did today was go shopping. I'm sure you can retrieve security cameras from the mall to verify the time I spent there. And while you're checking you will see that there was some man was following me. Then he approached me as I was leaving a store. Why don't you believe me?" Something much bigger and threatening was going on, and somehow she was right in the center of it. She looked at Marc, feeling more vulnerable than ever.

There was a knock at the door, startling Viv slightly. "That has to be Ralph," Marc said, as he walked toward it.

Ralph bulldozed his way through the door and looked at Viv. "Viv, we need to talk. Marc, will you give us a minute?"

"Sure," he said. "I'll be back in a few."

Ralph waited a minute and walked toward Viv. "Let's sit down in the living room."

She didn't argue with him. She wanted to see what his next move was going to be. Her resolution was firming as she'd had a few seconds to slightly gather her composure.

"I don't know what Marc has told you, but you're a person of interest in this ongoing criminal investigation. Before I take you down to Secret Service headquarters, I wanted to hear your side of the story."

She started to open her mouth, but he held up his hand silencing her. "Before you say anything, I need to tell you that you have the right to call an attorney. And if I was your friend, I'd tell you to do so."

"Are you going to have me arrested?"

"Depends on where the evidence takes us. Do you want a lawyer or not?"

"Ralph, I'm innocent."

"Then help me prove it."

"What do you need from me?" As she said the words, her hands shook.

"Let's back up to the night the President's campaign head-quarters were vandalized. Did you leave here that night?"

"No. I was in the whole night. I remember I was restless. Marc was asleep in the guestroom as usual."

"Can he vouch for you being here the entire night?"

"We were both asleep, but I didn't go anywhere. What, do you think I left my house, drove over there and vandalized the place? That is crazy! I'm the Senator's spokesperson for God's sake. Why would I ever do such a thing?" She shook her head in amazement at the accusations leveled against her.

"That's what I'm trying to figure out, Viv. You've been under immense pressure. First your mentor suffers a heart attack. Then you're thrust into the spotlight. You have some guy harassing you. He's murdered. That's a lot for any one person to take in. Maybe you just suffered a lapse in judgment." He reached over and patted her knee like she was a dog who had misbehaved.

Why did he think she was capable of such a thing? "I had no lapse in judgment. There's nothing to tell you about because, as I said already, I didn't do anything. I don't know who that is on that security tape, but it sure as hell isn't me."

"Marc told you." He raised his eyebrow.

"Yes. Do you realize how many people in this town have Georgetown hats? That's not evidence against me."

"You're right. Not by itself. But Viv, I can tell you, it looks just like you."

She threw up her hands. "There has to be a mistake."

"Okay enough about that. What about today?"

"I'll tell you just like I told Marc. I left headquarters around one, but I'm not sure exactly the time. Then I went to the mall and shopped until I got the call from Marc and came home. I'm sure there's security footage of me entering and exiting the mall, and I have my receipts. And to add to your list of items for your investigation, some strange man was following me around at the mall. He tried to talk to me, and I told him to get lost. But now I think there was something more to it."

Ralph narrowed his eyes. "A man was following you?"

"Yes. A man."

"And you didn't go anywhere near the Chamblee Hotel?"

"No. I did not," she said, careful to keep her voice even. She stared into his eyes and didn't look away.

"I want to believe you. Before I do anything, I'm going to verify your whereabouts at the mall and run prints. We already have yours so there's no need for me to print you again since you're in the system."

"Well I am the Senator's chief campaign spokesperson, and this is a presidential campaign," she said, not hiding the derision in her voice.

"I get it, Viv. And I will be the first to apologize if you get cleared, but we have to pursue the leads we have and they currently lead us straight to you."

She noted to herself that he said, if, not when. "What happens in the meantime?"

"Marc will stay here with you."

"I'd like to make a call."

"To your lawyer?"

"No, to my ex."

Ralph raised an eyebrow. "You're free to make whatever calls you want. Just don't leave your place without Marc. I'll also send over a sketch artist later today for you to work with to help identify the man who approached you at the mall. Got it?"

"Yes."

She walked into her bedroom and closed the door. She pulled out her cell and dialed Scott. Yeah, he hadn't been the best boyfriend, but he was still a friend. A friend who was talented in covert ops and she needed him. She hoped he wasn't deployed.

On the second ring, his familiar deep voice answered. "Viv. Wasn't expecting to hear from you."

"Scott, I need you."

"Well since you say it that way, I'll be right there. Didn't realize we were at that point just yet, but if you need a quick romp, I'm down."

She could tell by the light sound in his voice he was smiling.

"No, seriously. I'm in trouble."

"What's wrong?" His tone quickly changed.

"I shouldn't get into over the phone. Where are you?"

"I'm actually on leave. Doing some rehab, so I'm stationed at the Pentagon. Desk job. Sucks. You're worrying me, Viv. I'll be right there. You at your place?"

"Yes. And there's another man here."

"Do you need to call 911?"

"No, it's not like that. I'm being accused of something I didn't do. Related to some of the news you may have seen regarding the campaign. They've stuck a security guard on me. I need an ally. I can explain more in person." She felt herself gushing and tried to take a breath.

"I'm already in your neck of the woods. I'll be there in less than ten minutes."

She sighed and hung up. She might not want Scott as her boyfriend, but right now she needed someone who she could trust to be on her side. And for that, she could think of no one better.

Viv walked downstairs, and found Marc looking through her shopping bags.

"Are you going through my stuff?"

"Was just looking to see if I could find anything to help you. You failed to mention this receipt." He held up her lingerie receipt and the tiny pink bag.

"Can I have no privacy?"

"Viv, this receipt is from one forty-five. It's important. This builds out your timeline."

"Are you my defense lawyer now?"

"Believe it or not, I'm trying to help you." He walked toward her and grabbed her hands.

"You can help me by believing in me."

"I do. That's why I'm trying to gather evidence to help you. But you need to be honest with me."

The knock at the door had her on the move.

"Are you expecting someone?"

"As a matter of fact, I am."

She opened the door and Scott Ranger walked through it and picked her up off the floor with ease, giving her a huge hug and a smack on the lips.

"Viv, what in the hell is happening?" Scott asked.

"I was about to ask the same thing," Marc said, standing in the foyer with his arms crossed.

The two men eyed each other for a moment, neither one of them backing down. Maybe this wasn't such a good idea after all, but it was too late now.

"Scott Ranger, this is Marc Locke."

They didn't shake hands. They just stood sizing each other up.

"Marc Locke, why does that name sound familiar?"

"Marc's military too," Viv piped up.

"Really?" Scott said, his eyebrow raised.

Marc took a step closer to Scott. "I've heard all about you, Scott. Scott the SEAL."

Scott narrowed his eyes, still surveying the situation. "Viv, can we talk for a minute?"

"Definitely." She turned her attention to Marc. "Please stay down here and stop messing with my stuff."

"Yes, ma'am," Marc said.

Viv grabbed Scott's hand and took him upstairs to her bedroom.

"You've got a lot of explaining to do," he said.

"I don't even know where to start." She sat down on the edge of her bed.

His green eyes grew darker with concern. Those eyes used to get her every time. But not anymore. She needed a friend. And not just a friend, but a friend who could navigate this situation. She spilled the whole thing, from the time the flowers were sent to what happened a few minutes ago at her condo. She left out the fact that she'd slept with Marc. He didn't need to know that.

After she finished, he sat for a minute, brooding, and rubbed his chin. "Can you trust this chump downstairs?"

It was obvious that Scott had formed an immediate dislike for Marc. "He says he wants to help me. And I believe him, but I'm in over my head. The fact that they claim the footage looks like me makes me think someone is trying to set me up—or the Nelson campaign—or both. And now they have Marc stuck to my side twenty four seven, the Secret Service ordered it. So what the hell am I supposed to do?"

He grabbed her hand. "I'm glad you called me. We'll figure this out."

"Thanks."

"So what's the deal with the muscle downstairs? He has a military background?"

"Delta Force. Now he has his own private security firm."

"Ah. Delta turned security guard. Typical. Does he have any personal connection to the Senator?"

"No. I think he was hired because of his great credentials."

"Let me do some digging on him. Check him out. What about the Secret Service guy, Ralph?"

"I think he's a good guy. Trying to do his job. He hit on me at the very beginning, but he has since totally backed off. He's been extremely professional ever since the stalking."

"That loose end on the stalker bothers me. This guy stalks you and turns up murdered. Something doesn't add up. Then mix with that what is going on with the President's campaign, and some creep hanging around in the mall. This could be a lot bigger than you, Viv."

"That's exactly what I'm afraid of."

His serious expression turned into a smile. "I don't suppose that…"

"No." She laughed. "It's really not the time to make a move, Ranger. You had your chance, and you blew it."

"Aren't you telling me? Now I see you on that TV looking gorgeous as ever and talking policy issues, and it kills me. I was an idiot." He reached out and gently touched her cheek for a brief moment.

Just hearing that made her feel a little better. But she had no interest in picking back up things with him.

"All right. I'd like to have a chat with Marc, one on one, Army versus Navy, if you don't mind."

"That's fine. I'm going to take a long shower. Just please don't get into any fights, though, okay? Willow wouldn't appreciate the disruption."

"I'll do my best. Even though you know that cat hates me." He grinned and walked out the door.

* * *

Marc grew impatient as he waited for that goon to finish talking to Viv. He didn't even know the guy, but he already hated him. Even if Viv hadn't told him how Scott had treated her, there was something about him he didn't trust. Yeah, he may be a SEAL, but his cheating on Viv made him immediately suspect. The jealousy was bubbling up inside of him as he thought of Viv calling this guy instead of turning to him. It was a very smart move on her part, but it still stung.

He heard footsteps and knew the SEAL was coming downstairs. He turned around and there he was.

"We need to talk," Scott said, with a scowl.

"Okay, let's talk." Marc could play this game all day long. He looked Scott in the eyes.

"The way I see it, you're making trouble for Viv. Viv doesn't deserve that. So you need to back off, and put your energy and focus somewhere else. Where it belongs. Not on an innocent woman."

"You done?"

"No. I'm not. Have you looked at her? Taken a good look? Not just the exterior? She's a sweet woman. Yeah, she may act tough and crazy about politics, but she's the most kind-hearted woman I've ever met. She'd never harm anyone."

"I absolutely agree with you."

"Then what's the problem?"

"The *problem* is that there's a videotape putting her at the President's headquarters on the night of the vandalism. The *problem* is that she left Nelson's headquarters today in direct violation of what she'd been told to do by the Secret Service. I'm not only supposed to be keeping an eye on her, but also protecting her. Because if someone is trying to set her up, that means she could be in danger too. And now there's some random guy hounding her at the mall. Who knows if that's connected?"

"What's your angle here, Locke?"

"I don't have an angle."

"Bullshit." Scott walked over to Marc. The two men were only inches from each other.

"I've told you everything."

"I don't believe that, and you should know this. Yeah, I screwed up my chance with Viv. But if you hurt her in any way, I will hurt you. I don't care if you're Delta or not."

"I get it," Marc said. He wasn't looking to fight this guy. At least not right now. "I'm going to run and get something for dinner. Stay with her until I get back." It was the closest thing to a peace offering he was willing to give the guy.

"All right."

***

The three of them ate the Indian food Marc bought in awkward silence around her kitchen table. Viv's stomach rumbled in protest. Normally she loved the spicy curry dishes, but right now nothing was sitting well.

After dinner, Scott told her goodbye and promised to do his own investigating. Just knowing that made her feel better. Marc was harder to read. She had no idea what was going through his mind. Once Scott left, she dove right in.

"You're uncharacteristically quiet," she said.

"You called in your ex. Nice move."

She couldn't tell whether he was being sarcastic or serious. "I did what I thought would be best to clear my name."

"He still cares about you," Marc said.

"I know, but he realizes there's no chance between us. Once the trust is gone, you can't just bring it back with good intentions later. I have no romantic feelings toward him at all. He has been a good friend, though."

His eyes narrowed, and she wanted desperately to get inside his head. She walked over to the sofa and sat down beside him.

"I appreciate your honesty with me today." He turned and faced her.

"I've got nothing to hide."

"Okay. Then I've got one more question for you."

She sighed. More interrogation. "Go ahead."

"Did you buy that red lacy lingerie with me in mind or the SEAL?"

She was not expecting that question. She looked down, and was about to say something.

He held up his hand. "Don't lie."

"I hadn't even answered you yet."

"All right. Go ahead."

"You."

"Me?"

She groaned. This was going to be embarrassing. "Yes, you. I bought it with you in mind, as kind of an apology for what I said in my office earlier today. You happy now?"

"Very." He leaned over and pulled her toward him. Then his warm lips were on hers.

She pulled back. "So you really believe I'm telling the truth?"

"Yes I do. My job is to protect you. Because someone is clearly trying to hurt you and the campaign. Viv, I know you didn't do those things but finding the evidence to show otherwise is challenging."

"Because if you thought I had, you wouldn't sleep with me?"

"No," he answered without hesitation.

His sincerity was obvious. She didn't think he would lie to her. At least not about this. She knew what she wanted. Comfort, affection, and passion. "Don't you want me to change then?"

His eyes lit up. "Hell yeah."

"Meet me in my room in five minutes?"

He nodded.

She went up to her room and was glad she'd already taken a shower. She put on the new lacy red lingerie and hoped she wasn't making another mistake. Right now she just wanted to forget everything and enjoy the rest of the night with Marc. Was that so much to ask?

Right on time, he showed up. Not wasting any time he'd already taken off his shoes and was unbuttoning his shirt. She walked out of the bathroom with her silk robe on and gently dropped it to the floor revealing the lingerie. When his eyes met hers, he stopped moving for a moment. She could see him taking deep breaths.

He threw off his shirt and crossed to her in two large strides. His hands and mouth were all over her. She didn't want to think. Just feel. And right now feeling his warm hands roaming down her body had her on fire. She heard herself saying his name, but she didn't even know what else she was saying.

Even though he'd wanted her in the lingerie, it didn't stay on very long. He moved the straps gently down her shoulders with his teeth, and then fully undressed her. He leaned down and whispered in her ear, "One more question."

Oh, God. What now? "Okay."

"When you told me no in the office, did you really mean it?"

"I didn't know what I wanted."

"And you do now?"

"Yes," she said with conviction. She could be making a huge error by giving herself to him again, especially in the middle of this madness, but right now it felt right.

"What do you want?"

"To forget about everything. Everything but you and me."

"I can handle that."

With each kiss and soft caress, he took her to another place. Given the quickness that they landed in the bed, she'd expected a fast romp but he had something else entirely in mind. He was taking his time. Kissing and learning her entire body. She knew it was just sex, but it felt like more. Wishful thinking of a woman who always wanted something more from the men she'd been with.

He pulled back a second and made eye contact. "You still with me, Vivian?"

She felt her eyes widen as he used her full name. Something about him saying it sounded so sexy. "Yes." And she was ready to take charge. She rolled on top of him and started kissing down his chest. Then she sat up, knowing she needed a condom. Sensing what she was doing, he helped her out. "In my pants pocket. I brought a few."

She laughed and retrieved a couple, putting them on the nightstand and giving one to him. She watched as he put it on, and she'd never wanted a man so badly in her life. She felt him as he entered her and that amazing feeling that only he seemed to bring to her. The first time hadn't been a fluke. They were really this amazing together.

When she sensed the first wave of pleasure overtake her, she didn't even feel like she was in her own body. The sensation was so intense there was nothing for her to compare it to. Her reaction only furthered his, and he wasn't far behind her.

She collapsed on his chest and eventually rolled off of him while she tried to catch her breath. Viv had no idea what she was doing, but she knew she was enjoying it.

CHAPTER EIGHT

Marc left Viv at headquarters to go meet Scott. When he had received the ominous call, he knew something was up. Scott had told him they needed to have a meeting alone as soon as possible. When Marc had suggested the coffee meeting, Scott agreed.

He felt a little unsure about this, and knowing that he was Viv's cheating ex didn't improve his opinion. It's not that Marc didn't trust him, but he didn't have time for games. When he walked into the coffee shop, Scott had beaten him there and was sitting in the back corner at a two-top table. Marc approached him and had a seat.

"You wanted to talk to me."

"Yes I did, Marc. Or should I call you Special Agent Locke?" Scott asked with raised eyebrows.

Shit. His cover had been blown. He should've known not to underestimate the SEAL. "What do you want?" Marc asked.

"I want to know what you're doing messing with Viv."

"She's over you, man. You need to move on."

"That's where you're wrong. Yeah, I screwed that one up, but she called me. She asked for my help. So right now, she's my friend and you're not. I don't care who you work for or who you are, but you've messed with her. Because of that you're my enemy, and you need to start talking."

Who did this guy think he was? He wouldn't be intimidated by this SEAL macho crap. "I'm not trying to hurt Viv. I'm trying to help her."

"I'm not buying." Scott leaned forward. "First question. Who are you investigating? I know what FBI division you're in."

"You know I can't answer that question," Marc said, keeping his tone even. Scott's green eyes flared with disgust.

"You can play this game if you want. Imagine what Viv'll think when she finds out you work in the public corruption division of the FBI. I'm about to walk out of here over to Nelson's headquarters and tell Viv who you are."

"No, you won't do that."

"Watch me."

"I'll have you charged with interfering with an active FBI investigation."

"Do I look like I care?"

Actually, he didn't. Marc had to make his next move thoughtfully. "What do you want that I can actually give you?"

"Is Viv the target of your investigation?"

"Target is a strong word."

"Dammit." He leaned forward in his chair. "Stop playing games with me."

"No one has been ruled out, but I have my theories."

"All right. That's a start," Scott said. He cracked his knuckles and continued. "So she had to be on your list of targets, but you've pretty much decided that she isn't involved. Then you get this totally unrelated investigation in which you're taking a backseat to the Secret Service boys. You also don't think she's involved in that, but you can't prove anything. Am I right?"

Marc didn't say anything.

"Great," Scott said. "So I need you to tell me what I can do to help Viv."

Marc hadn't been expecting that. He didn't know if Scott's motives were pure, but Scott had a lot of extra room to work with at the moment and Marc didn't. "Find out who really is behind the crimes against the President's campaign. Provide alternatives, motive. And, if you can, look into the mystery man from the mall Viv mentioned."

Scott nodded.

"I think we're done here, right?" Marc asked.

"Just one more thing. I don't know all of what's going on between you and Viv, but once she finds out you lied to her, you're toast, buddy. Just like me. Probably even worse."

Marc felt a flare of anger and tried to tamp it down. He didn't respond and instead stood up and walked away. He wanted to punch a wall because deep down he knew Scott was right, and it pissed him off. Once Viv found out the truth, she'd never trust him again. He probably wouldn't even be relegated to the friend zone like Scott. He'd just be banished to the shit list. And how could he blame her? He hated himself right now. And more so because he'd started to develop real feelings for this woman. Something he wasn't used to. He had to help prove she was innocent, and then he had to figure out a way to win her trust. He had a lot of work to do.

***

Viv received a cryptic call from Serena asking to meet and saying it was important. Marc was out, so she figured she'd send him a quick text so he wouldn't freak out if he came back and saw she was missing. She rolled her eyes thinking back to the last time she decided to run out to grab some food and didn't tell him. If Serena needed her, that was her top priority.

She walked down the busy street enjoying the fresh air. After a few minutes, she couldn't help but feel like someone was watching her. She looked around and didn't see anyone particu-larly threatening—lots of people in suits. Typical for inside the beltway. She had no reason to be afraid. Her stalker was dead. Still, it bothered her that she couldn't shake the feeling that something was wrong.

She was relieved once she saw Serena standing outside of the deli. She put the thoughts out of her mind.

"Hey," Serena said. "Thanks for coming."

Viv took a seat at one of the outdoor tables with a large umbrella covering it. "What's going on?"

"Remember I told you how serious things were between me and you know who?"

"Yeah."

Serena let out a breath. "Viv, I think he's cheating on me."

Viv's heart sank. "Oh, no. Rena, I'm so sorry. Are you sure?"

"He's been acting really strange lately. Leaving at odd hours. He claims it was for work, but I just don't buy it." Tears brimmed in her eyes.

She reached over and grabbed her friend's hand. "You deserve better."

"I am head over heels for this guy, Viv. I don't know what to do."

"You can't possibly stay with him." Viv leaned forward in her chair.

"I need to figure out the truth. That's what I have to do. For my own sanity. I want answers. I need answers."

"Sometimes the truth isn't pretty."

"I know. And I realize you understand, especially after what happened with Scott."

"What can I do?"

"Just listening is enough." A stray tear fell down her cheek. "How could I have misjudged him? I can usually spot the dogs a mile away."

"First, you need to make sure he's actually cheating. What if he is really just leaving for work? Given his job, that's totally possible. Figure that out first before you jump to what you're going to do." Viv looked across the street and got a chill. The silhouette of a man standing in front of the frozen yogurt store looked eerily like the man from the mall.

"Viv, are you okay?" Serena asked.

Viv snapped back to reality and focused her attention on Serena. "Yeah, sorry."

Serena nodded. "I was saying that you're right. I could just be paranoid. Everything is so high stress right now." Serena stared off. "And speaking of stress, I know you need to get ready for the debate. I'm sorry I brought you out here to deal with my problems."

"Do not even think of apologizing. You're my best friend, Rena. I'm here for you."

"I won't keep you any longer. Good luck tonight. We'll catch up on your love life later. Don't think I've forgotten." Serena winked.

Viv looked down at her watch and knew she had to get back. She stood and gave Serena a tight hug. Then she started the walk back to the office. After a block, a warm breeze blew her hair into her face. She brushed it back and scanned the busy streets. No one seemed like a threat. And there was no sign of the man she thought she saw. It was time to stop being irrational and focus on work. She was safe. It had just been her mind playing tricks on her.

Later that afternoon, she bounced around headquarters excited for the debate. She'd be out front and center tonight on all the news shows promoting Nelson's hopefully stellar performance. The Senator was a great debater, so she had high hopes. But she didn't put anything past the President. That woman was tough and very smart. She noticed that Marc had stepped out for a few minutes, but he was back. And he seemed to be giving her the eye. She couldn't figure that man out. The only thing she knew with certainty is that she wanted him in her bed again. And again. And again.

He'd put her under some type of sex spell, and she had no idea if it'd ever be broken. She'd be ruined for life if it couldn't. She considered for a moment if that was a bad thing. The problem was he was supposed to be fun. Who was she kidding? Feelings had been present since day one, and they'd only gotten stronger.

She just couldn't keep things light and easy. She knew that about herself, but she'd gone ahead with it anyway. She had no one else to blame but herself. She could've just stopped at the one time. But once she'd gotten Marc back in her bed for more, it was all over. She had to keep reminding herself, though. She was still her own woman. She could get out whenever she wanted. It just so happened that she didn't want out yet.

Marc walked over to her, his stride confident as ever. His dark eyes examined her closely.

"Yes?"

"When do we leave for the venue?"

"I leave for the venue within the hour."

"No can do, Viv. I've got to go with you."

"Really?"

He grabbed her arm gently and guided her into her office, shutting the door. "What's wrong?" he asked, looking genuinely interested. Her heart melted. Not a good sign.

"Nothing. This shadowing thing is getting old. I mean I like you and all, but I don't need you to do my job."

"You weren't complaining when I was shadowing you last night." He raised an eyebrow.

"Stop it," she said.

"Seriously, though. I'll give you space, but I need to be there. It's for your own good." He grabbed her hands, and she didn't back away.

"You still believe me?"

"Yes."

"Why?"

"Just going with my gut."

She let go and crossed her arms. "Or going with another body part."

"Hey, it takes two to tango, babe."

"Don't call me babe."

"That annoys you doesn't it?"

She frowned. "Have you told anyone about us?"

"No. If Ralph suspects something, he'll remove me from your security detail."

"Good. I'd prefer to be discreet."

"Always." He winked. "Let me know when you're ready. Give me a heads up, so I can change into my suit."

***

They reached the George Washington University auditorium and made their way through the extra heavy security brought on, no doubt, by recent events.

"Are you going to shadow me the whole night?" she asked.

"Yes, ma'am. What's first?"

"I need to go back to the Senator's ready room and talk to him. Put yourself to some good use and get us through this heavy crowd to get back there."

Marc was in his element. All business. Looking so amazingly handsome in a dark suit. While she would've had to push her way through the masses, his presence commanded attention. His masculine energy emanated from his body, drawing her closer. She sighed just thinking about being with him. She needed to transition into campaign mode. This was a huge night for the Senator.

When they got to the ready room, she turned and he stopped. "I'll wait outside to give you all some privacy."

"Thanks," she said. She was glad he understood.

She opened the door and the room was abuzz of activity. She looked and in the corner at the table sat the big three—Nelson, Arthur, and Abby. Across the room stood Governor Banks. The Senator's VP candidate was attending tonight as a show of support and to prepare for his upcoming Vice Presidential debate.

The Senator's eyes lit up when he saw her, and he stood up.

"Viv, what took you so long?"

"It's a mad house out there, sir. And I couldn't leave headquarters until I had all the media spots squared away."

"Great. How're you feeling?" He reached out and touched her shoulder.

"Ready to go, sir. How about you?"

"Feeling good. These two have been grilling me for days and the practice session last night went really well."

Arthur stood up. "You've reviewed the newest talking points, right? Any questions?"

"No. I think they're solid."

"Of course they are," Arthur huffed. "I wrote them."

"Enough sniping you two," the Senator said. He turned to Arthur. "Everyone already knows how wonderful you are. Put yourself to better use and stop telling us all again."

Viv watched Arthur look sheepish for the first time ever. The Senator usually didn't call him out on his monster sized ego.

Abby stood up and walked over to Viv. "You look amazing. Love you in the bright colors." Abby referenced Viv's royal blue blouse under her suit.

Finally it was game time. Viv took her seat in the private viewing room. Arthur and Abby would split up—one staying with her and the other headed into the crowd with Governor Banks. Viv had her laptop ready to go. She'd need to keep up with things in real time. There was a team of campaign workers all with computers. She'd given everyone tasks earlier, so each person had certain areas to focus on. It was all being part of a rapid response team. If there were any flubs by the Senator, she'd want to deal with them immediately. And if the President faltered, she'd also want to capitalize on that. In the social media age, everything was immediate. There was no room for hesitation.

Her eyes were glued to the screen as the two candidates walked on stage. The Senator looked dashing with his dark suit and maroon tie. The President looked poised as always in a navy pantsuit.

The debate unfolded, and while each candidate made strong points, there were no direct hits. It was as if both candidates were walking on egg shells and being overly polite. The President looked a little stilted or nervous and while the Senator looked good, he wasn't really scoring any points either. The political chatter got less and less as the hour and a half progressed. She followed the social media feeds which had already cast the debate as boring and too focused on dry details. Americans really wanted juicy debates, even though they would say they wanted details.

She'd have her work cut out for her in the post-debate media spin room, but she was up for the task. Four hours later, however, she was second guessing her readiness. She was dead on her feet and ready to fall in bed. Finally, the cameras were turned off, and she looked up and saw Marc waiting patiently for her. He still looked amazing. Granted he hadn't been talking for the past few hours to the media hounds and pundits. When he looked at her and smiled, she felt warm inside.

She walked over to him, and he patted her shoulder. "Great job, Viv. You must be exhausted."

"You have no idea." Her shoulders slumped.

"Let's get you home."

The once buzzing auditorium now only housed the last remnants of the media and campaign staff. "Weren't you bored to death?"

"No. It was actually pretty interesting to watch it all unfold. Even though everyone is saying it was a bore. I didn't think so. You handled yourself great after, too—I liked how you pointed out that the Senator gave the people what they'd been asking for. I like it when you tell it like it is. So many political types don't."

"Thanks. It's been a long night. I feel like I could sleep forever."

"Just sleep?" he asked in a low voice.

She laughed. "Tonight, yes. Just sleep."

"Okay. I can accept that." He winked.

He was so sweet. He even brought her a snack and tucked her into bed. Next thing she knew she was passed out.

***

Marc was wound up even after a long night. He decided to let Viv sleep while he strategized downstairs in the living room. He was running into dead ends—and he didn't like dead ends. In fact, he hated them. What was he missing? He'd been able to call in some more favors and had reviewed the police report from Oscar's murder. He'd also gotten his hands on the autopsy. This kill wasn't just a murder. It had professional written all over it. It was clean, precise. Oscar was stalking Viv. Why? And who would want him dead?

Oscar had to be working with someone else. That someone killed him. Meaning Viv was still in danger. Was it someone who had something against the Senator? Or Viv personally? As far as he could tell, Viv really didn't have enemies. Everyone loved her. Even in her new role, she was a media favorite. What really bothered him the most was the possibility of this being connected to the vandalism against the President's campaign. Could they really be isolated events? Once again, he thought not. But that would mean someone was unhappy with both candidates. And with that assumption in place the list of possible suspects was substantially narrowed.

He'd also tried to do some intel gathering on the possible mall suspect. Based on the sketch artist's rendering, he worked all his sources. If the sketch and vital description was even close, he didn't fit anyone in the system. Maybe the guy was just a random creeper, but he'd been in this business long enough not to believe in coincidences. He also trusted Viv's instincts. On the day when the President's hotel war room had been ransacked, this mystery man had his eyes on Viv the entire afternoon. That meant something.

He sat down the beer he'd pulled from the fridge and leaned back on his sofa. At least for tonight, Viv was safe. He'd do everything in his power to make sure she stayed that way.

***

"We need to escalate things. Make it more interesting," the man said.

"Now? Don't you think we should wait?"

He slammed his hand down on the table. "You take orders from me. Not the other way around."

"I know, sir. I was just trying to give you my opinion from a strategic perspective. Shouldn't we keep our eye on the long game? The ultimate goal?"

"Tell me what you had in mind."

"One more scare, before something more major."

"What about the girl?"

"We've got eyes on her all the time. It's up to us whether we take her out or make her part of the master plan since she was a late addition to the game. I'm thinking she could provide us with more deniability. A better fall guy. Or girl. Depending on how it plays out we can pin it on the girl or the Senator. Or both."

"I do like the sound of that. Framing them both. No loose ends that way. Assuming it goes as I think it will." *Yes*, he thought. This could make things more interesting. He did tend to get bored easily.

"Of course, sir. We can make sure of that. Just give me a little more room to maneuver. Then we'll make the big play, and it will all be as you wanted."

"Make this work, and maybe I'll promote you to something very intriguing when the time comes."

"I'm counting on it, sir."

"All right. Don't bother me with any operational details. Do what you need to do, understand me?"

"Fully."

"You're a good soldier. Don't let me down."

CHAPTER NINE

Viv was glad it was the weekend. Yeah, her job was never done, but she didn't plan on going into the office on Saturday so she could recuperate from a crazy week. The Senator would be rolling out new messaging on Monday so she was laying low over the weekend as to not over saturate the market. He had other surrogates speaking for him on the Sunday shows. She was going to take the much needed opportunity to enjoy a bit of normalcy, or at least try.

Fortunately or unfortunately, part of normal meant dealing with Marc. He had practically moved in with her. She couldn't quite figure him out—or decide what she really wanted. Besides the obvious. She still wanted him physically. The sex only got better each time. She didn't even know it was possible. Did he want to be in a real relationship with her? They hadn't talked about anything like that. It was weighing on her, and she wanted to bring it up. Soon. It didn't have to be this weekend because she selfishly wanted more time with him without any relationship talk.

Marc went to go get dinner, and she sat curled up on the couch with Willow and a book. He'd asked if she wanted to go out, but really all she wanted to do was spend time alone with him. She felt a nudge and realized she must have fallen asleep. She looked up into his now familiar dark eyes.

"I didn't want to wake you but also didn't want the food to get cold."

"Oh, you did the right thing." She sat up on the sofa and felt her stomach growling. "What's for dinner?"

"Italian." He smiled and brushed a stray hair behind her shoulder.

Her heart warmed. She leaned in and kissed him, but he quickly pulled away. "If we start that, then I know the food will get cold." He grabbed her hand and pulled her up from the sofa, leading her into the kitchen.

"You want red or white wine?"

"What are we eating?"

He laughed and rubbed his chin. "I might have gone a tad overboard. I got chicken marsala, veal picatta and two types of pasta—one white, one red sauce."

She giggled. "All right. Let's go with the red wine."

They sat down to eat and a few minutes passed in silence. But it wasn't the awkward type of silence she'd felt on dates before. This was a comfortable silence that seemed natural. He hadn't opened up that much about himself, and she wanted to know more.

"Do you think you'll stay in the security business?"

He looked up at her. "Why do you ask?"

"I don't know. We're always talking about me and what I've got going on. Thought it would be nice to talk about you."

He averted his eyes and took a bite of bread. "There's nothing exciting about me to talk about. You know everything that's going on right now."

"Do you have a long term business plan?"

He grinned and leaned back in his chair. "Are you trying to run my business now just like you do with the campaign?"

"No," she said quickly. "I'm just curious."

"Well, I don't have a long term anything plan."

She didn't like the sound of that. He was basically telling her to back up. Was this just about the sex? Heck, if that's all it was, she'd just have to learn to deal because she wasn't ready to give him up.

He reached out and gently touched her hand. "But I like what I'm doing, so I can see myself doing it for a while."

She let out a sigh and focused on her pasta. She was going to let him initiate the next topic of conversation.

"What's your long term plan?"

She was surprised he'd asked her that. "Hopefully it involves working for President Nelson in the White House for eight years."

"And if that doesn't pan out?"

She felt like a deflated balloon. "Actually, I don't know. I haven't allowed myself to think like that. Have to stay positive."

"Politics isn't exactly a positive enterprise," he said smugly.

"So what's the deal? Why your extreme distaste for everything political?"

He waited a half beat too long before responding. She had hit another nerve.

"When I was in the military, I saw up close and personal what harm politicians can cause."

"What are you talking about?"

"Military action is often a political football. Each party tries to grab onto it and use it to its own advantage. But those same politicians don't have to live the reality of war. They don't have to face the loss."

Her heart broke for him. There was obviously more he wasn't saying but he was opening up more than he had before. She didn't want to push too hard. "It's always different for those on the front lines."

"Yeah. And I just don't like it when decisions are made based upon political calculations."

"Are you glad you left the military?"

"You may technically leave, but you're never fully out of the military. I left part of my soul back there in the desert."

This man sitting across from her now had faced some true hardships. She couldn't even imagine what he'd seen and done while deployed, but she respected all of his sacrifice. She squeezed his hand and didn't want to let go.

She tried to lighten up the conversation as they finished the meal.

"So I didn't get any dessert," he said.

"Well then I figure we can just have each other." She stood up and walked over to him. Then, she sat in his lap.

"That's the best idea I've heard in a long time."

He stood up from his chair holding her in his arms. His physical strength always amazed her. Tonight she'd also seen his emotional strength. It only made her want him more.

She laughed. "You can put me down."

"Yeah, but it's more fun this way."

She couldn't let this man go. How could she ever go back to the way she'd been before? His warm hands roaming over her body snapped her back to the present. She couldn't live in the future. She wanted to live in the now. She needed to live in the now.

"I don't think I can make it to your bedroom," he said, his voice ragged.

He sat her on the edge of the kitchen counter. She heard herself purr, and he started removing her clothes. She gripped his strong biceps and gently nipped at his shoulder. Too many clothes. She started to undress him.

It didn't take long before they were both naked. Her breathing picked up as his hands started wandering down her body.

"God, I want you," he whispered in her ear.

She grabbed onto him, urging him closer to her.

He swore and pulled back. Grabbing his pants off the floor, he pulled out a condom. She was glad he had been thinking because she was lost in the moment. He was the only thing on her mind.

He lifted her up off the kitchen counter and backed her up against wall with her legs wrapped snugly around him. She was overwhelmed by his strength as he held her. And then he was inside her. That glorious feeling of him filled her up. There was no slowness or tentative movements this time. He was taking her just the way she wanted him to. Hard and fast. Right now the faster the better. This Marc wasn't gentle or reserved. He was hungry and determined. She met his gaze and saw raw need. Knowing that she was having this amazing impact on him made her feel even more emboldened. She could tell he was losing control and sensing that made her entire body tingle.

"You're killing me," she said, out of breath. She gripped onto him even more tightly. As he drove inside her, she felt his desire for her through his movements, pushing her closer and closer to the edge with each thrust.

Her body took over, and she enjoyed a rush. Calling out his name, she dug her nails into his back—sensations rocking her body. Sensing him enjoy his own release made it even better. His breathing was rough in her ear as he held her securely against the wall. She could feel his heart beat pounding against her chest.

"Now let's go to the bedroom," he said softly.

Could he be feeling the same thing she was? This was more than physical. As much as she tried to tell herself it was just great sex, she now realized that was a lie.

***

Viv felt exhilarated after her weekend with Marc. She was ready to take on the world. She wasn't even bothered when Marc walked into headquarters with her that morning. At her desk, she reviewed the final copy of the new messaging points to prepare for her interview. She wasn't exactly looking forward to facing Steve Scrubbs again, but this time she'd be more prepared for his sneak attacks. There were a lot of things he could ask her about, and she'd be ready.

She went into the main room to watch the news to make sure she had a flavor of what was going on this morning. Viv walked into the room and her eyes went to the screen. There weren't many people milling around yet on Monday morning. She settled in a comfortable chair, and picked up the headphones so she could hear more clearly. After about ten minutes of catching up on the news, she was about to pull off her headphones when none other than Steve Scrubbs broke into the newscast. Immediately she knew something big was happening because he wasn't scheduled to come on this early in the day.

Her heartbeat picked up as she listened in to Steve speak, his face reddened.

"This is a rapidly developing situation I'm about to tell you about, folks. Literally unfolding minute by minute, but we have a confirmed report of shots fired this morning at the President's campaign headquarters. There is one confirmed campaign worker shot. We do not know the status of this worker, and we don't know if other shots were fired. The suspect is still at large. I can report to you that the President is safe at the White House. I repeat, the President is safe at the White House."

Viv threw the headphones off. She looked around the room and didn't see Ralph but saw Marc talking to another Secret Service agent at the other end of the room.

"Marc," she called to him.

His eyes met hers across the room, and he quickly walked over to her.

She pointed. "Look. Look at the TV."

He focused his attention on the TV. "Is this all they're reporting?"

"This is all I've seen so far."

"When did it happen?"

"They didn't say yet." She took a deep breath.

"At least you have me as an alibi."

She looked at him and saw the concern in his eyes. "What's going on here?"

"This just got a hell of a lot more serious."

"I can't believe someone was shot." Chills went down her arms.

"Yeah."

She looked up, and saw Ralph jogging over to them.

"We're stepping up security here. We need to shut down the office except for a skeleton security crew. I just sent out the message to everyone." Ralph narrowed his eyes at her, and she wondered what he was thinking. "Viv, what's your schedule?"

"I was supposed to do an appearance with Steve on CBW today. Given this happened, I don't know if he'll even want to do it. And if he does, I'm sure he'll want me to talk about this, not about the new campaign messaging which was the whole point. Obviously, this is awful. I'm sure the political minds on staff will have strong views on how we handle this."

"We all have our roles to play. The Secret Service is here to provide security. I don't give a rat's ass about the political element." Ralph went over the loud speaker and announced a shut-down of the office.

She waited for him to get finished speaking. "I understand that, I was just warning you that locking down headquarters may not be that easy."

"Point taken." He frowned as Arthur burst out of his office, and Viv knew a confrontation was about to occur.

"What the hell do you think you're doing?" Arthur asked Ralph. "We've got a presidential campaign to run here!" Arthur's voice exploded.

"I understand that, Mr. Rubio." Viv knew Ralph meant business when he started calling Arthur Mr. Rubio. "But I am tasked with the safety of this campaign and the Senator. That is my priority. We have at least one person shot at the President's campaign headquarters. Information is still coming in. This is a fluid situation. Until we know more, no one leaves here without security escort and all personnel will be escorted home."

"Unbelievable! You do realize the impact this could have on our campaign?" Arthur asked, his face reddening.

Ralph crossed his arm. "It's not my place to make political calculations."

Arthur slammed his fist down on the nearby table. "You can't do this."

"I can and I am." Ralph stood defiantly daring Arthur to further challenge him.

Arthur huffed and puffed, pacing around the room. "I need to call the Senator."

Ralph nodded. "He's probably being briefed as we speak, but it's a good idea that you call him."

Arthur didn't even respond to Ralph and walked into his office slamming the door. That left Viv standing with Ralph and Marc. Her head spun. Just when she thought things couldn't get any crazier.

"Hey, Viv. You okay? You're looking a bit pale?" Ralph asked.

"I think it's all hitting me. I'm just so confused. Are we really in danger? Who is the target?"

"I think that's what everyone wants to know," Marc said.

"We're working on nailing down the timeline and a massive Secret Service contingent is on the ground investigating. For now, Marc should get you out of here."

"I agree," Marc said.

"What about my interview at CBW?"

"Cancel it," Ralph said without hesitation.

"I don't think Arthur's going to like that."

Marc piped up. "The news is going to be all over this. I doubt you'd get to say anything you wanted anyway."

Her shoulders slumped. "All right. Whatever you guys say, but I'd like to let Arthur know."

"Don't worry about him. Security trumps politics. Always. If he gives you a hard time, let me know."

Viv nodded and walked to Arthur's office and knocked on the door. She walked in and he motioned for her to sit. He was on the phone, presumably with the Senator.

"It's ridiculous," Arthur said. "Yes, he told me that. I can't believe you're agreeing to this."

Viv surmised that the Senator had sided with the Secret Service. She wasn't surprised. This was deadly serious.

Arthur hung up and looked down. "We're getting crushed here, Viv."

"I know this doesn't help us at all, but someone was shot. We have to recognize how serious this is. If we run out there and keep yapping about campaign politics, everyone will turn against us."

Arthur rubbed his chin. "We're losing. And this awful attack only increases support for the President. Now we can't even counter. The Senator wants us to stand down."

"Ralph told me to cancel my spot with CBW, so I couldn't go anyway. That's what I came to tell you."

"Viv, if we don't get control of this soon, we're DOA. This election will be over. If you have any brilliant ideas, I'm all ears." He slumped down in his chair.

Wow, Arthur must be desperate if he was really seeking her input. "I'll give it a lot of thought and let you know. They want us to exit the building with security."

"I'll be done in a few."

She walked out thinking that she'd never seen Arthur look so defeated. All the momentum they'd gained was being sucked away. She felt defeated too. There was a small piece of her that was relieved, though. Marc hadn't left her side over the past twenty-four hours. She couldn't be fingered for this attack.

She stared at the TV for a moment, and they ran the same clips over and over. Then her stomach dropped. No, it couldn't be.

"Marc, Ralph!"

They both ran over to her where she was standing in front of the large monitor.

"That's the guy from the mall." She pointed to the TV. She tried to take a deep breath and put a coherent sentence together. "Those people running from headquarters. That guy, he's in the group running with those other people."

"You're saying he works for the President?"

"No, I'm saying he's the shooter!"

Marc and Ralph exchanged glances. Ralph nodded. "I'm going to call this in. Viv, if you're right, this could be a huge break."

"That's him, Ralph. I'm certain of it."

"I'm on it. You two get out of here."

Marc stood there waiting for her, and they walked in silence out of the building. Once in his truck, she let out a huge sigh.

"What's on your mind, Viv?"

"I don't like all these puzzle pieces that don't fit together. There's something big going on here. Who is trying to figure that out?"

"Multiple agencies. With the Secret Service taking the lead."

"Do you think they're up for that?"

"I do, actually. But I think there's something very strange going on. I'm disturbed about your stalker and the picture of you on the video footage. Why try to frame you?"

"Okay, what do we know? We know I had a stalker. The stalker was killed. I was framed for vandalizing the President's head-quarters. Why? And who killed the stalker? And now this guy following me is there when the shots are fired at the President's headquarters. You can't tell me that's not something."

"This latest incident is much more violent. If there's any evidence that attempts to tie you to it, we'll have something more to go on."

"But I haven't been out of your sight. You know that."

"Yes, but these people or person doesn't know that. They have no way of knowing the real story between us. So there's still a possibility that someone could try to frame you for this. Think, Viv. You don't have to be the shooter. You or a Nelson campaign operative could've hired someone. You could have even met the shooter in the mall. What if they have pictures of the two of you in close proximity? That could be the play if they try to pin it on you or the campaign."

"I'm in danger, aren't I?"

"I'd be lying if I said no."

She nodded and her head throbbed.

He reached over and grabbed her hand, keeping one hand on the wheel. "I'm here for you, Viv. We'll get through this."

"I sure hope so."

***

The guilt was starting to eat at him. He really wanted to come clean, but doing that wasn't an option at the moment. He was so screwed. Not only would she not trust him, their relationship or whatever you wanted to call it, would be over. He'd also not be able to protect her. He was torn. He felt like he wanted to tell her the truth—get it all out there. The repercussions would be huge.

The problem was that the truth would eventually come out, and then he'd be screwed then too. If he kept his mouth shut now, at least he'd be able to watch over her. He didn't want to freak her out, but he feared for her life. She could identify the mystery man who she'd seen at the mall and at the shooting. They might come after her next. He had no idea who "they" were.

By the time he and Viv got to bed, she was exhausted. The mental agony of everything was taking its toll on her. Now lying in bed with her, he had his arms wrapped around her tightly, and he listened to her shallow breathing. At least she'd fallen asleep. It was he who was lying awake.

Guilt wasn't even his biggest problem. He had racked his brain going over every scenario and trying to figure out what he was missing. What was the ultimate goal of whoever was behind this? Was it the campaign or something more?

Not having answers drove him crazy. He hoped that Scott had something because right now all he had was pure speculation. As much as he wanted to hate the SEAL, he was praying that he would come through. Anything that he could work with right now would be a weight lifted.

What would the perpetrator get from setting up Viv? Hurt the Nelson campaign and that would assure the reelection of the President. Then what? Who was the most motivated for that to happen? These attacks on the President's campaign did give the President a bump and made the Nelson campaign look bad.

He'd contact Scott tomorrow and hope he had something more. Right now, he was basically fighting blind.

The next day, Marc called Scott over to Viv's condo. When Scott walked through the door, Marc pounced.

"What did you find out?" Marc asked.

"Where's Viv?"

"She's in the shower. Talk quick if there's something you don't want her to hear."

"I'm hitting massive dead ends. Whoever's behind this is good. Really good. And they know how to cover their tracks. This man Viv identified as being the mall guy is a phantom."

"A professional?"

"Something like that." Scott rubbed his chin and sat down on the couch. "He simply doesn't exist. He's hired by someone, and we don't know who that is either. Whatever this is, it's big. Now with the shooting, things have really taken a turn for the worse."

"I hear the President won't back down and wants to do the joint appearance with the Senator tonight at the charity event. Viv has to be there."

"That place will be crawling with security, but if my hunch is right, it won't matter. I don't have the Secret Service cache behind my name, but I think it's a bad idea."

"I hear you, but you'll never keep Viv from going."

"Keep me from going where?" Viv walked down the steps, her eyes narrowed at both of them.

"The joint appearance."

"Damn right. This is a big event for us. The Senator is the one who presented this idea to the President. We have to be there. I have to be there." She stood with her hands on her hips in defiance.

"I already told Scott that you were going. I know there's no talking you out of it."

"Scott, what do you think?"

He leaned forward. "I think you should stay far away from both campaigns."

She laughed. "You do realize it's my job? That's like telling you to stay away from the field. I understand the shooting impacted everyone. But because of that, security is going to be the tightest it's ever been. We'll be safer at that event than anywhere else in the world."

***

Viv thought that Marc and Scott were overreacting. Yeah, she was freaked out about the shooting at the President's campaign headquarters, especially with the mystery man still at large, but tonight was a charity event, an event she'd been helping plan for months. There would be tons of security—both Secret Service, local police, and private security like Marc.

She got dressed for the charity gala. It was black tie, and she put on her favorite cocktail dress. She hated little black dresses, so she made her own fashion statement with a candy apple red dress. It was strapless and fitted through the top with a flare skirt.

She couldn't afford to be looking over her shoulder every second. She had a campaign to win. That's what Marc was for. She knew he'd protect her. He'd pulled back a little. It was subtle, but she'd noticed. She couldn't say she was surprised. She knew things weren't going to last forever, but she had been hoping it would have lasted for a bit longer. She'd started developing strong feelings for him, so maybe in the long run it would be better this way.

Viv walked down the steps and standing there waiting for her was Marc. Not just regular old Marc, though. This was Marc in a classic black tux. He looked astoundingly handsome, so much so, that she thought for a brief second about jumping him in her living room. But then she thought better of it.

"Wow, Viv. You look beautiful. I'm almost speechless." Marc's eyes were blazing and only warmed her up even more.

"You look pretty amazing yourself."

He walked over to her and wrapped his arms tightly around her. She thought he was going in for a kiss but instead he leaned down and whispered in her ear. "Are you sure I can't talk you out of this?" He pulled back and looked down into her eyes.

"You know you can't."

Then he kissed her, and she briefly thought he could convince her to stay in tonight. But the event and all it represented was a lot bigger than her needs. She really believed in this charity gala. A combination of different charities would benefit, including each candidate's spotlight charity: a children's hospital for the Senator and a rape crisis center for the President.

She broke off the kiss. "We should be going. I don't want us to get distracted."

"I'm going to be all over you tonight."

She raised her eyebrow. "Can't that wait? I don't think that's very professional."

He laughed. "I didn't mean it like that. I meant I'm not letting you out of my sight. I know how important this is for you, but you need to let me do my job just like I'm letting you do yours. All right?"

She nodded. She didn't know how this would play out at the event, but there was no use in arguing about that now.

They arrived at the five-star Terrace Hotel and were met with more security than she'd even expected. Even with all of their credentials, it took them twenty minutes to get through the security line. By the time they were inside the large ballroom, she was exhausted.

"Well that was an experience," she said. "I told you the security would be crazy here. See, nothing to worry about."

Marc didn't smile. His eyes told the story. He was on guard. Could he really think something was going to happen after what he'd just seen? She chalked it up to his military background and focused on why she was there. The Senator was set to make his big entrance soon followed by the President. The media were out in full force, and she'd need to be on her game.

Ugh, she thought. Just what she needed. In the mass group of media representatives emerged her favorite talking head, Steve Scrubbs. He claimed to be a news anchor, but he editorialized far too much for her liking. He was headed straight toward her, and she wasn't the least bit surprised.

"Vivian Reese," he said as he grasped her hand and shook it. "I'm sorry you had to cancel our interview, but under the circumstances I understand. Awful, isn't it?"

"Yes, Steve. It is awful."

"Any comment about security at the event tonight?"

"As anyone who is here knows, including yourself, security is a top priority of both campaigns." Out of the corner of her eye, she saw Marc who had stepped back giving her ample room, but he wasn't that far away.

"Yeah, yeah. I understand that. But don't you think it's a risk to show up at an event like this given the shooting at the President's campaign headquarters just occurred?"

"This is a very important event for some amazing charitable causes. We can't yield to senseless violence. We must continue on and show whoever is doing this that we don't give up. We're all Americans after all. These charities need this exposure, and the Senator is happy to be here tonight providing his full support."

"Speaking of that. Any chance I could get a word with him?" He paused. "Please."

"I'll see what I can do. And, Steve, make sure you make a donation tonight."

He raised his eyebrows.

"To the charities."

"Ah, yes. Of course." He smiled and walked away.

Marc was by her side again. "I think that Scrubbs guy was hitting on you."

She laughed loudly. "I doubt it. That would be a strange approach."

"Would you like anything to drink?"

"I would, but not now while I'm working the room. Last thing I need to do is make an alcohol-induced flub."

"Just thought it might take the edge off."

"Do I seem on edge?"

"A little tense, but that's understandable."

She didn't feel that tense. "Maybe you're the one on edge. I feel fine. I would like to run to the restroom before the Senator and President get here."

"All right." He put his hand on her back and started leading her toward the restroom.

"Marc, you know you can't go in there with me." She couldn't help but laugh. "I'll be fine."

"I'll be right outside by that small bar area." He pointed to a bar near the restroom hallway.

She nodded and walked away from him. She really just needed a moment to compose herself. Examining herself in the mirror, she made sure everything was in place. She added some more lipstick and took a few deep breaths. Everything was going to be all right.

As she exited the ladies room, her pulse quickened. The man—the mystery man, or someone who looked a lot like him, walked out of the men's room and back toward the crowded ballroom area. This man's hair was much darker, but the build was strikingly similar. Could he have dyed his hair? He turned around briefly and made eye contact. Her heart constricted. His face was expressionless, but his hazel eyes piercing. Could it be the same man?

She quickly turned around and saw Marc talking to the bartender. Hurriedly she walked over to him and grabbed his arm pulling him away.

"What's wrong?" he asked.

"The man—the one from the mall. I think he's here."

"Are you sure?"

"No," she sighed. "I can't be sure, but it really looked like him. His hair was a different color, but the face and build looked so similar."

"Which direction did he go?"

"Back into the main crowd."

"I'll let Secret Service know to be on the lookout for a possible suspect."

"What about the event?"

"They're not going to call it off if you can't give a positive ID."

Her heart sunk. It surely seemed like the same guy. But what if it wasn't? Yeah, he could've changed his hair color, but there were hundreds of men here tonight in tuxes that could fit his general description. There was so much security here she had to have faith in that even if his eyes were still haunting her.

"I know they won't call it off, but you'll report it anyway?"

"Of course."

She felt her phone buzz, and she saw a text message from Abby indicating the Senator was making his entrance and to meet them before he did. "The Senator's here. We have to go."

They weaved their way through the crowded room to one of the side doors. Once they reached the door, she walked through it. She saw the Senator standing alone with Abby and Arthur.

"Viv, you are looking well," the Senator said. "I'm so glad we didn't have to cancel this event. I know you've worked so hard on pulling it all together."

"Thank you, sir. Me too. The donations have already started coming in. It should be a great night." She couldn't worry the Senator with what she'd seen. Or what she thought she'd seen.

"Now, of course, I have to go in before the President makes her entrance. Are we ready?"

Arthur nodded. "Yes, sir. You'll make one trip around the room. Shake some hands, we'll make sure you get the right photo ops with the charity reps, then take your seat at the head table."

Viv stayed close to the Senator as he worked the room like a pro. The President entered the room only moments later looking stylish as always in a long black demure gown that fit her tall and slim stature perfectly. Her auburn hair swept into a wispy up-do. Still, the Senator was still getting a lot of attention which was a good sign in her book. If everyone had flocked to the President, then she would've really started to worry. She'd seen the latest polls. Their bounce had dissipated, and now they were trailing again. They needed momentum.

The President started walking directly toward her.

"Hello," the President said.

"Madam President," Viv replied. Viv wondered what was going on. What would the President want with her?

"I just wanted to meet you, Ms. Reese. I've seen you on TV now numerous times, and I have to say I'm quite impressed."

Viv was at a loss for words. "Please call me Vivian. And thank you for your kind words."

"I know we're political opponents, but it's so refreshing to see a strong young woman jump into the political fray." The President's hazel eyes twinkled. "You remind me a bit of myself when I was young."

"Coming from you that means a lot."

The President reached out and gently touched her arm, leaning in closer to her. "Please be careful. I don't know what is going on out there, but I fear we all could be in danger."

Viv nodded, and the President took a step back.

"If you ever decide that your party isn't treating you right, give me a call."

The President smiled and turned away, leaving Viv in a state of shock. She couldn't believe what had just happened. She didn't know if she was more surprised by the compliments or scared by the warning.

Viv took a deep breath as she watched the Senator take picture after picture with the great charity representatives. He was a good man. He would make an amazing president. She had nothing against President Riley, but she didn't think she had the right vision or the best policy positions.

Each candidate slowly made their way up to the head table. They wouldn't be sitting beside each other because that seemed too awkward—both campaigns had agreed on that. There would be a buffer of key people from the charities sharing the table. Viv would be seated at a table close by and would be keeping her eyes on things at the head table.

She was slightly regretting turning down Marc's offer for a drink. Everything seemed under control. It would be a long dinner without any wine. Maybe just one glass. She sat down, and Marc took the seat beside her with a clear view of both the Senator and President. She almost jumped when he grabbed her hand and squeezed it under the table. She wasn't expecting that. She had totally fallen for this guy. She'd gone and done exactly the last thing she wanted to do.

She picked at her salad and accepted a glass of wine poured by the server. Marc ate in silence, his eyes constantly surveying the room. Marc was probably amped up because Viv thought she saw the guy who was following her at the mall. Given all the security, she felt as safe as she could. It was clear he didn't.

Like most fancy dinners, she knew she was in for a multiple course affair. When they brought the lobster bisque, she checked her watch and saw they'd already been sitting at the table forty five minutes. It was going to be a long night.

***

Marc didn't like the feeling deep in his gut. They'd made it through an excruciatingly long meal, and now it was time for the Senator and President to say a few words over desert. He hadn't seen anything out of the ordinary besides the President talking one-on-one with Viv. He couldn't wait to hear the story on that.

Security was crawling all over the place, so he couldn't explain why his instincts were telling him that the shit was about to hit the fan. Maybe it was being in the field for all of those years. He might just be paranoid. It didn't help that the Secret Service hadn't been able to locate anyone fitting Viv's description. A slice of chocolate cake and a cup of coffee weren't going to ease the feeling that something bad was going to happen.

He looked over at Viv. He hated that his apprehension had put her alert too. She smiled at him, and when he looked into those blue eyes he felt a fierce twinge of protectiveness. The last thing he wanted was for her to get hurt.

The Senator's speech was quick and effortless. Filled with humor, Marc had to admit that he really connected to the crowd. As the President approached the podium, he noted the Secret Service presence. He should just take a deep breath and make it through the short remarks. Then hopefully he could take Viv home and spend the night in her warm bed.

President Riley smiled and adjusted the microphone. "I'm so glad that everyone could make it out tonight to support these wonderful causes. Tonight is a night to celebrate not what tears us apart, but what brings us together."

A huge round of applause broke out, and he could tell that even though Viv smiled with her lips she was frowning with her eyes. The President was a formidable force, a tall and graceful presence matched with a brilliant mind.

President Riley continued. "I urge everyone tonight to think about more ways we can work together to support…"

It all happened so fast. The President slumped over the podium. Screams rung out. Holy shit. Was that blood? Had some-one just shot the President of the United States?

Mass chaos broke out. His first thought was of Viv, but he also knew he had an obligation to the Senator. Secret Service swarmed around the President and the Senator. He wasn't going to be able to get through them, so he focused on Viv. She looked shell shocked and pale.

"Come on," he said as he grabbed her arm. "Let me get you out of here."

"The Senator!"

"He's fine. He has his own detail on him."

"The President? What happened?"

The noise in the room was deafening. People were crying and yelling. Everyone was trying to get to an exit. He had to make sure Viv didn't get trampled. He protected her with his body, and there was no way he was going to let anyone get to her. Bodies swarmed around him, and he could feel her shaking under his touch.

He leaned down and whispered in her ear. "It's okay, Viv. I've got you. We're going to get the hell out of here."

She nodded weakly, and he kept guiding her to the closest exist. Luckily the large hotel ballroom had multiple big doors. All things considered, it could've been much worse.

How had someone gotten in a gun to shoot the President? He didn't hear or see a thing. All he had was his gut feeling. He should've trusted it, especially once Viv told him she thought she'd seen the mystery man. But what was he supposed to do? The Secret Service had made clear to him that they weren't calling off the event. It was already the tightest security of any event to date. Whoever was responsible was skilled. And deadly. He just hoped the President would make it.

* * *

Later that night, Viv sat on her sofa next to Marc, still confused and scared. An attempt on the life of a sitting President was mind boggling. She wasn't thinking about the campaign or politics. She was thinking about being an American. The source of pride she felt for the country overwhelmed her. She prayed the President would survive. The news outlets were going crazy, but the administration was very tight lipped about the President's condition. A news conference with the Vice President was supposed to come on the national news at any minute.

"How're you holding up?" Marc asked as he gripped her hand.

"Honestly, I don't know. Things have escalated to a point I could've never imagined. Attacks on property are one thing. Then the shooting at the President's headquarters. And now this? I don't even know how to process it." She leaned her head against his shoulder, and he ran his hand through her hair. "The Secret Service should have done something. The man I saw must have been the shooter."

"Viv, we don't know that. You said yourself that he didn't look exactly the same. The best we can do is to let the Secret Service do their jobs. Do you need to call your people again?"

"No. Last I heard, Arthur decided to only put out a written statement tonight. For once I agree with his decision. We need to understand how the President is doing first. That is the top priority. Not the campaign."

"Even for Arthur?"

"He might be a lot of things, but he would never advocate violence against a sitting President." She looked up at Marc. "You can't seriously think he could be behind this?"

"You did say he'd do anything to win."

"Yes, well, first, he's not a killer. And second, this wouldn't be the right move to win. Everyone will rally around the administration now. So put that thought out of your head. No one in the Nelson campaign could be behind this. No one." She didn't back down. Whoever did this, they were not working for the Senator. She believed that with every fiber of her being.

"I understand how you feel."

"But you don't agree."

"Honestly, Viv, at this point, anyone could be a suspect."

"Including me?"

"You know I didn't mean that."

She sat up straight when she saw the TV flash with Vice President Brett Meyer walking out to the podium. "Shh," she said. She turned up the volume and focused all her attention to the Vice President. It looked like he was fighting back tears.

"First, I want to report to the American people that President Helen Riley is in stable condition."

Viv felt herself let out a huge breath of air. Thank God the President was stable.

He continued, "She is being treated by the best doctors in the world. All I can tell you now is that she sustained a single gunshot wound to the shoulder. Every American can go to sleep tonight knowing that her injury is not life threatening. I will work tirelessly to make sure we continue to run this country day-to-day." He took a deep breath and looked directly into the camera—his dark eyes glistening. "And now let me send a message to whoever is responsible for this heinous and terroristic attack on our President. We will find you and bring you to justice. To the wonderful citizens of this country. We will persevere. May God bless you, may God bless our President, and may God bless the United States of American. Good night."

She turned away from the TV to look at Marc, and he was frowning. "What is it?" she asked.

He ran his hand through his hair. "My brain is on overdrive right now. I don't think I'll be able to sleep."

"Me neither."

"Come here." He pulled her gently into his arms and laid down on the sofa. Just feeling his strong touch made her feel safe. But was she? Was anyone? If they could shoot the President, clearly they could kill her. It wasn't her they wanted, though. Or at least, not right now.

Her cell phone buzzed, and she started to sit up.

"Do you have to get that?" he asked.

"Yeah, I do." She found her phone and answered. "Hello."

"Viv, are you all right?" Scott asked.

"Yeah. A little shaken up but I'm fine."

"Is there anything I can do?"

"Not right now." She looked over at Marc who narrowed his eyebrows. He obviously wanted to know who she was talking to.

"Is Marc with you?"

"Yes."

"Good. You know how to find me if you need me."

She hung up and put her phone down. "That was Scott."

"Do you still have feelings for him?" he asked quietly.

"What kind of question is that?"

"Don't I have a right to ask?"

She felt tired and defensive. "No, I don't have feelings for him."

He crossed his large arms over his chest.

"I'm going to bed," she said. It had been a hell of a day. She didn't want to end it with a needless fight.

"Not alone, you aren't."

She studied him. He was jealous of Scott. She didn't know whether to be happy or mad. She walked up toward her room, and he followed closely. Truthfully, she was glad he did. She didn't want to spend the night alone. Hopefully tomorrow would be a better day.

CHAPTER TEN

Two days later Viv sat at campaign headquarters surrounded by the Senator, Arthur, and Abby. The current debate was how to respond now that they knew the President was going to live. The latest report was that she'd have to do some rehab for her shoulder, but it wouldn't impact her ability to run the country. That meant the election was still on, but how long did they need to keep the gloves off after an assassination attempt?

"I think we wait a week or so," the Senator said.

Arthur groaned and leaned back in his chair. "Senator, a week might as well be a year in this election. I was on board at the beginning. We obviously needed to make sure that the President was going to be fine, but now we know she is. We're already in a hell of a hole. She'll have a ton of sympathy votes. Not to mention people thinking it's patriotic to vote for her."

"That's exactly the point," Abby said. "That's why we need to be seen as supportive and rallying around the flag right now. We still have time. We're a month and a half out."

"Viv, what do you think?" the Senator asked.

"Isn't the answer always somewhere in the middle?" She spoke confidently. "We don't want to be out there in everyone's face today on the cable outlets, but we also can't be forgotten. Arthur has a point that if we let things get too out of control, we'll never be able to make a comeback."

Arthur smiled at her, obviously shocked that she somewhat sided with him in this fight.

"Sir, Viv should try to set up a visit with you and the President at the hospital. That will be good PR. I doubt her people would turn us down because that would make them look bad."

"Good idea." The Senator stood up from the conference room table. "Our Secret Service detail is really urging everyone to be on alert. So I wanted to remind you that we still don't know exactly what is going on here. Everyone needs to be vigilant."

The door to the conference room swung open. Ralph and other Secret Service agents stood along with local police and men in FBI flak jackets.

"What's going on?" the Senator asked.

"I'm sorry, Senator." Ralph walked over to where Arthur sat. "Mr. Rubio, you need to come with us."

"What is this about?" Arthur demanded.

"I don't think you really want us to get into that here," Ralph said quietly.

"Like hell I don't. What is it?"

"We're bringing you in for questioning in connection with the assassination attempt on the President."

"This is crazy," the Senator said and walked toward Arthur. "What evidence do you have?"

"We're not at liberty to discuss an ongoing investigation, Senator. I'm sorry."

"I want to call my lawyer," Arthur said.

"We understand," Ralph replied. "But you have to come with us now."

Viv sat at the table, unmoving. Shocked. This couldn't be happening. When she had told Marc that Arthur couldn't be behind the attack, she had meant it.

The agents ushered Arthur out, leaving the three of them stupefied. The Senator began to pace while she sat in silence at the table.

"We need to get on top of this. I'm going to call my lawyer too." Abby took off her glasses and shook her head. "Just when I thought things couldn't get any worse. Arthur may be a son of a bitch, but he's not a killer."

The Senator rolled up his sleeves, and Viv could see a tiny bead of sweat forming on his brow. "Don't you think I know that?" he snapped. He pounded his fist on the table in a rare show of anger. "Someone is trying to screw with us, and I don't like it one damn bit."

"They're trying to make it look like our campaign is behind the attack," Viv said softly.

She met the Senator's eyes and knew she had struck a nerve. "Damn right, they are, and I'm not going to stand by and let an innocent man be destroyed. This is about a lot more than my campaign. Arthur has dedicated his life to politics and for the good of this country. He doesn't deserve this. Meanwhile the real threat is still out there."

"I know, sir."

"Viv, do everything you can and try to get me a meeting with the President. It's now more important than ever."

"Will do."

"And watch your back. I don't think we can trust anyone at this point."

Sadly, she felt like he was right. Could she even trust Marc? She was about to find out.

* * *

What the hell was happening now? Marc watched as Arthur was escorted out of campaign headquarters by an entire group of

Secret Service and FBI agents. Luckily, no one he knew. The last thing he needed was for someone to blow his cover. At this point though, his original investigation was shot. He'd already gotten a call from Peter that he was to assist in any way possible with the current security efforts. Obviously an assassination attempt and ongoing campaign threats outweighed his campaign finance angle. He hadn't found any additional evidence showing campaign finance impropriety. This made him wonder whether the initial evidence was planted.

Did the Secret Service really have something on Arthur? Or was this a total shot in the dark? He feared that they'd want quick answers—someone to put the blame on. If they thought Arthur or the Nelson campaign fit the bill, then who knows how it would play out.

His chest tightened just thinking about Viv being in danger. His stress level was also mounting over their ever intensifying relationship. His feelings were rapidly growing for her, but he knew that as soon as he came clean he would be toast. What if they decided to bring her in for questioning? It wouldn't surprise him. They could go after both her and Arthur. Heck maybe even the Senator himself. The whole thing smelled rotten to him, and he didn't like it.

He watched as Viv walked out of the conference room. Her expression was unreadable.

"Let's get out of here," she said quietly.

He nodded and guided her out the door and to his car. Once they got in he spoke. "What was that?"

"That was Arthur being taken in for questioning. Someone or multiple people are after us. They're trying to take down the Senator. A really screwed up way of trying to do it, but I think that's the end game here."

"You really think so?"

"Yes. I do." She crossed her arms over her chest.

"Then why attack the President?"

"I'm still trying to figure that one out," she said loudly. "But she's not dead, is she?"

"Whoa. You're really getting into conspiracy theory type ideas here, Viv." His mind raced, analyzing Viv's accusations.

"Am I? I don't think it's that far-fetched."

He looked over at her for a second and then turned his attention back to the road.

"You think I'm crazy?" she asked

"It's not that. I know you're not involved. And you really seem to believe Arthur's not, even though you can't stand the guy. Could there be anyone else? What about the…"

"No," she cut him off. "The Senator is innocent. The whole team is innocent. You need to come up with some new theories." She pulled out her phone and started dialing.

"Who are you calling?"

"Scott."

"Why?"

"Because he'll listen to me."

He gripped the steering wheel tightly. "I am listening to you. I just think you're wrong."

It ticked him off that she was going back to Scott for help. He listened to the one-sided conversation, one that included her inviting him over to her place. He couldn't help the pang of jealousy that shot through him.

They rode the rest of the way to her condo without Viv saying another word. He didn't know how things had gone from so good to so tense between them in such a short time. She was under a lot of stress, and he tried to remember that. Nothing about their relationship had been normal, but he couldn't stop the strong jealous urges he felt towards Scott. Would she go back to him? It was surely possible. Scott had gone a long way to redeem himself.

He thought it better not to push his luck right now. She was worked up about Arthur, so he should lay low. But there was no way he was going to leave her alone with Scott. They walked inside her condo, and he went into the kitchen and poured Viv a shot of whiskey. Maybe that would take the edge off. He poured himself a double. He knew her routine well enough to know that she was in her room probably changing out of her suit and into one of her Georgetown sweatshirts. He didn't want to sleep in the guestroom tonight.

A knock at the door let him know that his SEAL friend had arrived. Reluctantly, he walked over to the door and opened it.

Scott walked through the door and then turned to face him. He frowned. "Where's Viv?"

"In her room."

"You still haven't told her, have you?" Scott asked accusingly.

"No. Still not the right time."

"There's never going to be a right time. You realize that you're going to hurt her worse the longer you wait?"

"You don't understand."

"Yeah, I do. I'm an asshole piece of shit just like you are when it comes to women. I've made a lot of mistakes—the biggest one was with Viv. Don't give me crap about it not being the right time."

Surprisingly, Scott's honesty didn't piss him off but actually made him respect Scott a bit more. "Man, I know I'm screwed, all right?"

Scott nodded. The conversation stopped when Viv walked into the room. She was wearing the sweatshirt just as he predicted. She'd pulled her hair back into a ponytail.

"I poured you some whiskey."

"Thank you." Her expression remained passive.

"I'll give you guys a minute." He didn't plan to stay gone too long though.

***

Viv hated to see him go, but she couldn't let her feelings get in the way of what she needed to do.

Scott stood up from the sofa and walked over to her. "What's going on, Viv?"

"I don't know. I need someone who will hear me out."

"I'm listening. Here, sit down."

"Do you want anything to drink? You may need something to get through this."

He paused for a second, and she took that as a yes. She went to the kitchen and poured him a decent amount from the bottle Marc had left on the counter. It was just a whiskey type of night. She took a deep breath and went back into the living room trying to gather her thoughts to be able to articulate her ideas.

"Thanks," he said, as she handed him the whiskey. "Just lay it on me."

She looked at him sitting comfortably on the couch, and she realized how she could've fallen so hard for him. He was incredibly attractive. His dark blond hair was currently cut short, and his green eyes were always so full of life. But right now, in this moment, she wasn't attracted to him. Not in the way she used to be.

"The Secret Service took Arthur in for questioning, but I know he's innocent. In fact, everyone in the Nelson campaign is innocent."

Scott leaned forward toward her. "How can you be so sure?"

"I know these people. I know the Senator. He's practically a father to me."

"Whoa, back up. I never accused anyone of anything. I was just asking."

"I know," she muttered. God, she was tired. She pulled her hair down out of her ponytail to release the pressure pounding at her temples. "I wish I could explain this better." She took a deep breath. "We're being set up."

"Who?"

"The Nelson campaign."

"But the President was the one who was shot."

"Yes, and now Arthur is being questioned. Someone is trying to pin all these attacks on us. It will guarantee the President wins re-election."

"Aren't there easier ways to win elections? No need to take a bullet." He raised an eyebrow.

"I know that's the piece of the puzzle that doesn't make sense. But it's clear to me that someone is trying to frame our campaign for these events."

"And you called me because you thought I'd believe you?"

"Not just that. I want your help. Your ideas."

"What about your Delta man?"

She sighed. "It's complicated."

"You really like him."

"Sometimes he infuriates me. Like with this current situation. I know that he's in a tough spot, but I just want him to support me and have my back. He keeps questioning everything."

Scott laughed and then took a sip of his whiskey. "Babe, he's Delta. What can you expect?"

"I know. I should've never gone there in the first place. I wasn't thinking."

"Sometimes not thinking is a good thing."

"I can't believe you're defending him."

"No, not defending him. I'm defending your ability to let loose. Have fun. You're such a serious woman, Viv. You have a right to not be sometimes." He reached out and gently touched her cheek.

Marc walked back into the room, and his eyes were ablaze. He obviously thought something was going on between her and Scott. Nothing could be further from the truth. To Scott's credit, he didn't try to escalate things.

"So what do you think about Viv's theories?" Scott asked.

Marc took a few steps into the living room and sat down in a chair. "I know Viv wants to believe in the people she works with, but something doesn't add up."

"Why does that automatically mean that Arthur is guilty?" she asked.

"I didn't say he was guilty." He paused. "But I also didn't say he was innocent."

"Like I told you before, hurting the President in any way hurts us too. Arthur isn't stupid."

"She's got a point there," Scott said.

"Then what's your theory, SEAL?"

"I don't like to speculate before I've done a proper investigation."

She turned to face Scott. "Well then, would you?" she asked.

"Would I do what?"

"Look deeper. See what you can come up with." She paused and looked him directly in the eyes. "Please."

"Sure. I'll let you know what I find." He stood up from the couch. "I'm going to call it a night. I'll let myself out."

She sat on the sofa, and Marc stood from his chair and walked toward her. "Okay if I sit beside you?"

She felt her defenses starting to break down. "Yeah." Why did this man have such a grip on her heart?

"Scott's being helpful."

"I'm glad to see you two aren't fighting."

"I don't want you to be upset with me. I'm sorry if you are. That was not my intention." He reached over and placed his hand on her knee. She knew exactly where this was going. Straight to her bedroom.

"Let's not talk anymore about it tonight."

He murmured something under his breath that she couldn't understand. The next thing she knew he grabbed her hand and guided her to the bedroom. She couldn't comprehend why she felt so right with Marc when everything else was so wrong. But for now, she was going with it.

He was so strong, but always gentle with her. It was like he could read her mind and knew exactly what she needed from him. She sat down on the bed, and he ran his hand softly down her cheek. Was this what it was like to really be in love? The feeling hit her like a brick. With a fierce longing for him she pulled off his shirt and ran her hands down his chest and abs.

He nipped at her ears and neck, and she heard herself groan. She could never get enough of this man. As she reached to pull off her shirt, his hands gripped hers. "Here, let me," he whispered in her ear. Even though they'd been together multiple times, each encounter felt exhilarating in its own way.

She loved feeling the touch of her skin against his. He seemed so hot and hard against her cool softness.

"I can't get enough of you, Viv," he whispered as he removed the rest of her clothes. But he was in no hurry. She was the one filled with an unspeakable need for him.

"Hurry," she said, as she fumbled with his zipper.

"I'm not going anywhere." He quickly grabbed a condom from his pocket before removing his pants.

"I know, but I need you. Now."

He cocked his head to the side and grinned. She thought he might try to tease her, but instead he didn't break eye contact as he entered her slowly.

She closed her eyes for a second, taking in the heightened feelings.

"Look at me, Viv."

She did, and couldn't believe the look of desire in his eyes. Moving together in perfect rhythm she marveled at how quickly he had learned her body. They were so unbelievably connected that it didn't take long for the first wave of pleasure to overtake her. He refused to stop there. He drove her to the brink again, and this time he was right there with her.

"Viv." He groaned.

That was it for both of them. She felt another shock throughout her body.

He rolled off of her and pulled her toward him. She could feel his heartbeat, and wondered what it would be like to be with this man. Not just for today or next week. But forever.

* * *

Viv's condo had turned into command and control for what Marc liked to think of as Operation Nelson. If they didn't find out who was behind the attack on the President soon, the Nelson campaign was as good as done. That included Viv and all of her hopes and dreams. Marc wanted to do everything in his power to make sure that didn't happen. He'd gotten orders from Peter to stand down on the campaign finance investigation for the time being. There was too much going on with the current security threats. Once he'd filled Peter in on the fact that he hadn't uncovered any additional evidence of campaign finance wrongdoing beyond the initial email, his orders had been clear. Stay put, assist in the current investigations in any way he could, but don't meddle into the Secret Service's jurisdiction. Peter tended to agree with Marc that the evidence against the Nelson campaign was probably planted. But right now, security concerns trumped everything.

Well, he wasn't exactly meddling. He liked to think of it is as an independent outside investigation, and one the Secret Service never needed to know about. Between him and Scott, they could do a lot. As much as he hated to admit it, Scott wasn't all bad. Was he still jealous? Hell yeah. But Scott didn't seem to be trying to win Viv back, and Scott's instincts were very good not to mention his contacts. For now, they would work together.

He glanced over as Viv poured coffee in a mug. "You guys want some?"

Marc nodded and Scott sat quietly typing away in his laptop. He'd underestimated how smart this guy was.

"Scott?" she asked.

He looked up from his computer and smiled. "No. I'm good. I did find something you'd be interested in, though."

"What?"

"I've been digging through Arthur's financials."

"Is that legal?" Viv asked.

"This isn't being used in a lawsuit. This is our own independent fact finding mission."

She put her hand on her hip and raised her eyebrow. Damn she was sexy, and she was spending her nights wrapped in his arms.

"Anyway," Scott said. "There's absolutely no unusual activity. None. I've searched deep and wide. If there was large amounts of unaccounted for money either coming in or going out, I'd know about it."

Viv took a seat and drank a sip of coffee. "So you're saying that there's no financial evidence that would tie Arthur to the attack on the President."

"Exactly."

"And you think that if he was involved, there would be a money trail."

"Not so fast, though," Marc said. "This is good news. It supports Viv's theory that Arthur is clean." He looked at Scott. "But you and I both know that if he was skilled, he could hide it."

"Anything is possible. I'm just sharing what I've found."

Marc nodded. "Fair enough."

Willow jumped up onto Viv's lap. The cat hissed in Scott's direction. Marc couldn't help but laugh.

"That cat freaking despises me," Scott said.

"It's because she knows you don't like her," Viv replied. "Makes me wonder how you must have traumatized her."

"Maybe she just knows that Scott is trouble." Marc couldn't help the playful jab.

"Hey now. Let's focus on the issues."

Viv rubbed Willow's ears, and Marc enjoyed the one moment of normalcy amidst the insanity.

Viv leaned back in her chair and pulled Willow closer. "Am I going to have to say out loud what neither of you seems to have the balls to say?" Her blue eyes flashed with anger. "This assassination attempt reeks of an inside job. You saw the security at the charity gala." She looked at Marc. "There is no way someone could have gotten past there without some help on the inside. And by inside, I mean Secret Service. What if that mystery guy is connected to the Secret Service somehow?"

Scott sat forward and pushed his laptop down. "Viv, that's a pretty huge accusation."

"And why would the Secret Service try to hurt the President of the United States?" Marc asked.

"The same reason most people in this world are motivated to do bad things—money and power."

Marc didn't want to admit it, but Viv had a damn good point. He looked over at Scott and saw the wheels spinning in his head too. "If we start snooping around into the background of Secret Service personnel, we can't get caught."

"I don't plan on being caught. Do you?" Scott asked.

"Let's get to work then." Marc hoped they were making the right move.

CHAPTER ELEVEN

Viv sat in her office at campaign headquarters across from Marc seriously considering if they could have sex on her desk. He'd tried once before at the beginning of their relationship, and she'd said no. Relationship? Is that really what this was now?

He sat quietly, and in Viv's opinion sexily, as he brooded over some new security protocols that had come in.

Her door swung open and Ralph walked through, his face red.

"You." He pointed to Marc. "You are a son of a bitch."

Marc sat not saying a word and raised his eyebrow.

"Ralph, what are you doing?" Viv questioned.

Ralph didn't look at her and instead took a step toward Marc. Marc stood and they were toe to toe.

"I suppose I should call you a son of bitch, Special Agent Locke."

Marc's eyes widened with surprise for a brief second. "Why don't we talk outside?"

"What, you don't want your girlfriend to know that you've been playing her the whole time? Playing us the whole time? Just to further your FBI investigation?"

It was like someone had slapped her across the face. Stunned. She processed Ralph's words and looked over at Marc. When she saw the expression on his face, she knew it was true. Her whole world came crashing down on her. He was a liar and a cheat.

Marc turned to her. "Viv, let me explain."

Ralph blocked his path. "No. I'm sure she'll want her chance to bust your balls, but she's got to get in line because I'm first."

The room closed in around her. She had to get out of there. She ran out of her office and straight to her car. She didn't look back.

***

"Was that fucking necessary?" Marc asked Ralph. He was so mad that he was worried he might even strangle Ralph. Yeah, he should've come clean to Viv before, but Ralph had no business outing him like that. He was still an undercover Federal agent.

"You sure do have a lot of nerve," Ralph said. He started pacing back and forth in Viv's small office. "Did you think it would be funny to try to play the Secret Service? And to keep your relationship with Viv from me too?"

"This was never about the Secret Service. This was a campaign finance investigation. Something you have no interest in, nor any jurisdiction. I was just doing my job and following orders."

"Well, I suspect your boss may be in deep shit because my boss is pissed, and he's going for blood."

"I don't know what to tell you, man."

"Even if you originally needed your cover, once things got crazy and threats increased, you should have told me."

Ralph looked like he was about to lose it as he stood with clenched fists. Marc could take him if he had too, but he really didn't want this to resort to violence. "Just take it easy. I was following direct orders. I wasn't trying to make your life more difficult."

"If you ever cross me again, you'll wish you hadn't."

"Are you threatening me?"

Ralph didn't respond and walked out leaving him alone in Viv's office. Dealing with Ralph was the least of his worries. He had to find Viv. He wondered if there would be any coming back from this.

He carefully weighed his options. She'd be beyond pissed. If he went after her, he knew she probably wouldn't listen. A cooling off period might be wise. On the other hand, there may be no chance in ever having a shot with her if he didn't try to start doing damage control right now. This was worse than being stuck in the desert. When had he gone soft?

He ran out of the office and through the building. By the time he reached the parking lot, she was long gone, as he assumed she'd be. He could go over to her place, but she probably wouldn't let him in. And even though he had a key, it didn't seem like the approach to take right now. Would she call Scott? He hoped not.

Not wanting things to go into a downward spiral, he dialed Scott's number and hoped he got to him first.

"Yeah," Scott answered.

"I'm in deep shit."

"She found out," Scott said, his voice even.

"It was a first class cluster job."

"I told you it would catch up with you, man."

"I don't need a lecture right now. I just wanted to give you the heads up. She'll probably be calling you soon."

"How did she find out?" Scott asked.

"Ralph, the damn Secret Service guy, outed me in front of her. He got all territorial on me. Guess I shouldn't be surprised. I'd be pissed too."

"If I were you, I'd be a lot less worried about Ralph and his guys and more concerned about Viv. You already know how I feel about this whole thing."

"I hear you."

"If you want some good news, I have a little bit."

"All right." He would take the smallest piece of good news right now.

"My additional searches on Arthur all came up clean."

"And that's good how?"

"We can exclude him from our list of suspects."

Marc couldn't help but laugh. "Was he ever really on your list anyway?"

"He had to be, but now he's not."

"Keep digging. We need a break."

"We do. And you need a miracle."

"Screw you."

"I think I'm growing on you, aren't I?"

Marc couldn't help but smile because Scott was right. He had grown on him, kind of like a barnacle. And to be honest it had been a bit of time since he'd had a friend who got him. After losing his best friend and his Delta teammates, he had wondered if he even needed friends any more. His goal was to try and not make any new enemies. "Let me know if you find out anything else."

"Don't do anything stupid, Locke. You're already in the dog house."

Hell, he knew that. He just hoped he would be able to get out.

***

Viv threw back the whiskey without a second thought. Damn him. As the anger pulsed like fire through her veins, she could barely think. How in the world had she been duped? And in such a major way? Marc was an undercover FBI agent investigating the campaign, and by extension, her. She wanted to strangle him.

But even more than that, she wanted to find out what the heck he was investigating. She didn't know if it was connected to all of the recent events, or if it was something else. She knew one thing, though. She deserved answers. She'd slept with the man for

God's sake. More times than she cared to count over the past few weeks. Had it all been a ruse?

Her heart started to hurt, and she poured another shot of whiskey. Then she walked over to the couch and sat down. She needed to focus on being angry because she couldn't process any other emotion after learning of Marc's betrayal. She closed her eyes and took a few deep breaths. She wanted to call Serena, but she was worried that she shouldn't tell the whole story to her best friend. While she trusted Serena completely, the fact that she worked for the President did complicate things in a case like this. The last thing she wanted to do was to put her best friend in the position of knowing something about the Nelson campaign and not being able to say anything. She'd just have to deal with this issue herself.

"Wow," she said out loud. She thought the Scott cheating fiasco had been bad. But being lied to and used by an undercover government agent took things to a different level. Had it been Marc's plan the entire time to get her in bed and use her to further his investigation?

When she heard the knock at the door, she didn't want to move. Would he really have the nerve to show up at her house right now? She dragged herself off the couch. When she looked through the peephole and saw him standing there, she had to make a quick decision. Send him away or let him in and curse him out. If she was being honest with herself, she couldn't remember the last time she'd been so mad.

As she opened the door, he stepped through it. She was about to start in on him, but before she could open her mouth, he stepped toward her. She immediately stepped back, but he followed and then eased her up against the wall. He leaned down and pressed his lips to hers. For a moment she wanted to forget everything, but she couldn't. No. She had a shred a dignity left, and she wouldn't be manhandled or seduced. Gathering up all her strength, she put her hands on his chest and tried to push him away.

"You have some nerve, you bastard."

He took a step back and sighed. "I know. I've got a lot of explaining to do, but I'm hoping that you'll let me."

She looked at him. His dark chocolate eyes were pleading with her. She wanted to kick him out. On the other hand, she also wanted to know what he was doing. She had to give it to him. He had the nerve to show his face. She turned her back to him and walked into the living room. Yeah, she needed another shot.

She sat on the sofa and tried to give him her best "stay the hell away from me" look. He must have gotten the message because he took a seat in the chair.

"I don't know where to start," he said.

"I can help you with that." She leaned forward a little. "What are you investigating?"

"It's not what you're thinking."

"How would you know what I'm thinking?"

"I'm investigating campaign finance crimes," he said with a straight face. "In the Nelson campaign."

"You're what?"

"I know you heard me."

"That makes no sense. The Nelson campaign is one hundred percent clean. I can guarantee that. Is this a political stunt? Some of the President's lackeys must have gotten to the FBI."

He shook his head. "No, Viv. It's not like that at all."

She laughed. This was the biggest crock she'd ever head. Of course the President's people had to be behind this. "How freaking stupid do you think I am? Yeah, I know you fooled me, and I'm sure you must feel great about that. But c'mon. Treat me with a little respect."

"I'm telling you the truth. This is a totally non-partisan independent FBI investigation. The President has nothing to do with this."

"Even if it's not President Riley, her people are involved."

"No, they're not."

"That's completely unbelievable."

"It's true. Will you at least hear me out?"

She crossed her arms and leaned back in the couch waiting for his surely asinine explanation.

"I spoke to my boss on the way over here. I've been cleared to tell you the following information."

She wasn't liking the sound of any of this so far.

"We had credible evidence that there was funding and coordination between a certain Super PAC and the campaign. There is a paper trail. An email documenting a trade—contributions in exchange for a commitment once elected on certain issues. I'm not at liberty to say what those issues are right now."

"That's impossible. I'm telling you. Who in the campaign did this supposed email go to?"

"Well that's one of the problems. It's a general campaign email address."

"Sounds like a setup. Just like everything else has been. Someone has been trying to take down the Nelson campaign. This crazy FBI investigation is just part of the larger picture."

"I'm beginning to believe that myself. But you have to understand that I didn't have any of that specific knowledge at the beginning. I was sent in with the belief that there could be something illegal going on inside the campaign. My orders were to determine if there was any illegal campaign contribution activity. I wanted to find the truth."

She laughed. "Did the truth include sleeping with me?"

"Damn, Viv. You must know I didn't plan that."

"That first night we went out. You mean to tell me you weren't already plotting to get me in bed and find out all the campaign's sordid secrets?"

"I'll admit it, I was willing to try to get closer to you and gain your trust, but I had my boundaries. What has happened between us is real."

"How am I supposed to believe that when you've been lying to me from the start?" She felt her voice quiver, but the last thing she wanted to do was cry.

He stood from the chair and kneeled down beside the sofa, grabbing her hand.

She tried to pull away, but he didn't let her.

"What do you want from me?" she asked.

"I want you."

"What, am I just supposed to overlook the web of lies? Just say, hey, you're forgiven? It's all good? How can you expect me to do that? How can I ever trust you again?"

"I was doing my job. I was doing the best I could. And if it's any consolation, once I got to know you, I knew you couldn't be involved. When I realized that you were in great danger I did everything in my power to protect you."

Hot tears stung her eyes. "Just get out."

"Please don't do this."

"Don't make me ask you again."

"I'll leave for now, but I'm not just going to walk away. Not this time."

She didn't know what he meant, but she just turned her head from him. He stood up and walked to the door. When she heard it close, she let the tears flow freely. Willow sensed something was wrong and walked over to her. As she held tightly onto Willow, seeking comfort, she felt lost. What was she supposed to do now? She'd gone and fallen in love with a man who didn't even exist. She didn't even know who the real Marc was. Had it all been lies?

***

When Scott called and invited him for a beer, he thought Scott might rub his nose in the fact that he'd royally screwed up with Viv. But because he felt awful, he decided to go anyway.

He walked into the pub and Scott was already sitting at the bar with a beer in front of him.

"Hey, man," Scott said.

"Did you invite me here to gloat?" Marc sat down on the stool beside him and motioned to the bartender for a beer.

"Believe it or not, I didn't. To be honest, I really didn't like you to begin with, but now I think you did what you had to do. Convincing Viv of that will be challenging."

"Don't I know it? I just saw her this afternoon."

"You want something stronger than a beer?"

"No. What I need is a solution."

"Give her some time. Put yourself in her place. You'd be in a rage right now if the tables were turned."

He nodded and knew that Scott was right. "I know that logically, but it doesn't make it any easier."

"You've really fallen for her, huh?"

Marc downed a good part of his beer. "Yeah."

"Why don't we talk about something else?"

"Fine by me."

"Tell me the real deal about why you left Delta."

That might be an even worse topic than what had happened with Viv. "Kicking a man while he's down is never nice."

"Before you give me a load of crap about retiring and all that you should know that I've already heard the rumors."

Marc slumped down a bit in on the stool. "Maybe I do need something stronger than a beer."

"That's more like it." Scott ordered them both some whiskey. They sat in silence until the bartender placed the two tumblers in front of them. "Okay, out with it."

"It's complicated."

Scott laughed. "Isn't it always? I have enough complicated SEAL stories to last all night. But you go first."

Marc considered his options. He knew he couldn't go with his usual cover story. He could either tell a sanitized version or tell the truth. He looked over at Scott's piercing green eyes, and made the call. He was going to just spit out the truth.

"I made a decision in Afghanistan. That decision got one of my teammates killed. The other Delta members turned on me, even my best friend. At that point, there was no way I could stay." There, he'd said it. The thing he hadn't said to anyone.

"What kind of decision did you make?"

Marc leaned in a bit closer to Scott. "I made the call to go after the number two Al-Qaida man operating in the province at the time. I knew it was dangerous, but I didn't see it as a suicide mission. Every decision in the field is a judgment call."

"Man, I know that. So what happened?"

"Everything went to hell. It was a setup. The intel turned out to be bogus. When we went into the village that night, there were enemy combatants waiting for us. One of my guys was literally blown away. Three others injured. Me and my best bud were pretty banged up, but the only lasting impact I suffered was the fact that everyone blamed me."

"I don't understand. How could they blame you?"

"I'm the one who brokered the bad intel. I had a source that I thought I could go with. I was the only one in the group who believed the lead was solid. My buddy fought me on it, but I finally pulled rank. That decision got our teammate killed. The injured were bad off. The three of them will never be in top condition again. All because of me."

"You made the best call you could. A true friend wouldn't turn his back on you like that."

"Well there's one more piece to the story."

"All right."

"The guy who got killed was my best friend's younger brother."

"Shit." Scott finished his whiskey and patted Marc's shoulder. "God, I'm sorry."

"Me too. So that's why he hates me. I killed his little brother."

"Dammit, Marc. You didn't kill him, those terrorist bastards did."

"That's not the way my buddy saw it. I made the call. I disagreed with the rest of the team, and I used my position of authority to do it. At the end of the day, it's on me. I have to live with that every day for the rest of my life."

"So you left the military after that?"

"It was already the end of my tour. My team was evacuated from the field to receive medical care and to do a full debrief of the incident. I knew then that I could never re-up."

"When's the last time you talked with your friend?"

"We avoided each other. Then I called him to tell him I was leaving. He basically said go to hell, and that he never wanted to see or talk to me again. I wasn't even welcome at his brother's funeral back stateside." Marc's stomach clenched as he felt the fresh wave of pain just like it was yesterday.

Scott gave him a hard pat on the back. "Believe it or not, I understand. Have I lived your exact experience? No. But I can relate."

"Thanks." In a way it was a relief to talk about this. He'd kept it locked away and hidden every single day. Seeing a flash of understanding go through Scott's eyes provided a bit of comfort. Something he wasn't used to feeling.

"This type of stuff will kill you if you let it. Eat you from the inside out. I've seen it happen."

"Now you know the real story."

"Are you going to tell Viv?"

"Why would I do that?" Marc needed more whiskey. This was getting way too deep for him.

"Because you care about her. She cares about you. It'll help her understand you better—the real you. Isn't that what you want?"

"I don't want her to think I'm more of a monster than she already believes I am."

"What you are to her right now is a liar."

Marc grunted. "Thanks."

"I'm serious."

"I did what I had to do. Orders are orders. You know that."

"You didn't have to sleep with her. That wasn't an order."

Marc felt his face redden as his body warmed up. "You have a lot of nerve. You cheated on her."

Scott looked away.

"What?" Marc asked.

"I guess I can't preach honesty and then lie to you. I never cheated on Viv."

"What are you talking about?"

"I told her I cheated on her, but I didn't."

"Why would you have done that?"

"I got cold feet. Really cold feet. I was crazy about her, but I wasn't crazy about settling down. I liked her and didn't want to hurt her. I also knew that if I tried to break it off, I wouldn't have the willpower to stay away. So I made the story up of cheating on her and forced her to break it off with me."

"Hell and I thought I was screwed up."

"Yeah."

"So you want her back now?"

"No. If I still had feelings for her I wouldn't let you near her again, much less sleep with her. But I don't. In the end, I realized that we really weren't the best match. We're better off as friends. I think she knows that too."

"She will be pissed at you when she finds out."

"She won't."

"Won't what? Wait a minute. What about all this truth telling mumbo jumbo?"

"There's no need to tell her. She's moved on. It's better this way. But I think the two of you could work, like really work. If, and only if, you are honest. If you act like me, and keep lying, you'll never have a real chance with her. I'll consider telling her the truth after the two of you make up."

"That's if we make up. A mighty big if."

"Understood." Scott drained his beer. "What're we going to do about our other problem?"

"We need to figure out our next move. Viv and the Nelson campaign are still in danger. We also need to figure out who makes it onto our list of suspects."

"Any ideas?"

"Something just doesn't feel right to me. I've got that twitchy feeling I used to get out in the field."

"I'm feeling it too. It's off. What plausible scenario could there be for all of these events being linked? From the beginning when Viv got the flowers, up until the attempt on the President's life. I think we've lost sight of the bigger picture."

"I'm listening," Marc said.

"Who has the most incentive to see the President re-elected?"

"Besides the President herself?"

"Yeah."

The realization hit him. "No way. You think the VP is behind this?" he asked in a low voice.

"Listen. I think it's unlikely, but we're running out of scenarios. Think about it. The President is hurt. The sympathy vote basically guarantees re-election combined with the suspicion over the Nelson campaign. A suspicion that started with the acts of vandalism."

"Where does Viv's stalker come into play here?"

"I'm still working on that angle, but the fact that he was murdered suggests that he got out of line. Didn't follow the program."

"So your bottom line, best theory at this point is that the Vice President is behind this."

Scott waited then looked him directly in the eyes. "You got anything better?"

"No, but understandably, I'm not in love with that idea. What about some rogue Secret Service agents with an ax to grind?"

"I'm not saying it has to be the VP personally. Could be someone who supports his interests. Whether it be Secret Service agents or otherwise."

"Either way those are some serious accusations. And think about this. If the VP is involved, that means after the election the President could still be in danger. If he really wants to be President and is willing to take it this far. Imagine the next steps. We need evidence. Cold hard non-refutable evidence. Not just rank speculation."

"Exactly. And that's what we're going to get. By pooling our resources we're going to get to the bottom of this. I already started doing a bit of digging into some of the Secret Service agents that were at the charity gala."

"And?"

"Nothing so far. But you and I both know that these guys would be stellar at covering their tracks. And I'm still looking into this mystery guy that Viv mentioned."

"We may not have much time to try to figure this out." He shook his head.

"While we're working on it, you're going to spill your guts to Viv."

Marc laughed even though it wasn't that funny. "Great." Marc couldn't help but feel a tiny bit of relief from confiding in Scott. He wasn't so bad after all, for a SEAL.

***

Viv sat in her office at campaign headquarters with a raging headache and a heavy heart. Arthur was still a prime suspect in the attack on the President. She knew deep in her gut that he was innocent, but she couldn't prove it. At least not yet. They had gotten news that the President had been released from the hospital and was back at the White House. It was clear that her campaign was ready to push full speed ahead again, and this time they had a huge advantage. With the dark cloud of suspicion over the Nelson campaign, how could they even have a chance at making a comeback?

She'd have to be the one to try to sell the message to the American people. It seemed like such an impossible task, but the Senator refused to give up. She was going to present the idea to him that he needed to get out there in the media and start giving interviews. The public needed to hear from his own mouth that the Nelson campaign was innocent, and that he still deserved to be considered for the presidency.

A light knock on the door grabbed her attention. She looked up and saw Marc. Her stomach dropped. After yesterday, she didn't know what to do. She didn't invite him in, but she also didn't order him out.

He walked in and shut the door behind him. "Have a minute?"

"Didn't you say enough yesterday?"

"Actually I don't want to talk here. I was hoping we could talk tonight. There are a few things I need to tell you."

"Why can't you tell me now?"

"This isn't the best place to have the conversation."

That was curious. She wondered what he was up to this time. She was still angry with him and being in her office reminded her of all the reasons why she had a right to be. She felt herself clench her fists, but then she took a deep breath and slowly exhaled. He wasn't worth sending her into an even further stressed state.

"Please," he said. "I really do need to talk to you." He took a step toward her.

She wanted to move, but she didn't. He placed his hand on hers. Was this all part of his elaborate ruse? Her internal battled raged on, but in the end she knew she'd relent. "All right. But after tonight, that's it."

He nodded. She didn't believe that he would go away that easily. The sad thing was, she didn't really want him to. And she kind of hated herself for that.

***

"This was your bright idea," Marc told Scott under his breath as they wound their way through the White House.

"This is strictly recon. There shouldn't be any issues," Scott said.

"Famous last words."

Scott smirked, but Marc didn't respond. When Scott had called him up wanting to take a trip to the White House, Marc thought Scott had lost his mind. But Scott had been able to get a meeting with some of the Vice President's staff. This would be the perfect opportunity to talk to some of the VP's people and start making assessments.

"Remember the cover story. The impact of cyber warfare on the Navy."

"Man, I'm not one of your amateur SEAL buddies."

Scott laughed. "I guess not. But for today you are, and I outrank you."

Marc had agreed to take a lower rank and play Navy boy for the day. He was close enough to Scott's size that he borrowed one of Scott's uniforms. He hoped this didn't blow up in their faces.

When they reached one of the offices for the Vice President's staff, they signed in and waited to be greeted. Within a couple of minutes, two staffers walked out—one tall and blond, the other shorter and Latino.

"Lieutenant Commander Ranger, great to meet you. I'm Thomas Ring and this is Bruno Rivera."

"Thanks for having us. This is my colleague Lieutenant Gary Mixson."

Marc shook hands with both men. Both of their handshakes were too light for his taste, but he tried to stay focused on the mission. They were ushered into an office, and Marc mainly kept quiet while Scott and the two guys droned on about cyber warfare for nearly an hour. He was beginning to think it was a complete waste of time when the Vice President walked in.

"Mr. Vice President, please meet our guests from the Pentagon. This is Lieutenant Commander Scott Ranger and Lieutenant Gary Mixson. They're here talking about cyber warfare."

A flash of interest crossed the Vice President's face and that was quickly replaced by a smile. "Great to meet you two gentlemen. How can I help?"

"Actually I think we've made a lot of progress today. Not sure that there's anything else to discuss for now. Your staffers have been very helpful," Scott said.

Marc knew it was now or never so he dove in. "Yes, thanks to you both. Mr. Vice President is there any way we could have a word with you in private?"

The Vice President raised his eyebrow, but then nodded his head quickly. "Of course. Thomas and Bruno, thank you again. I'll let you debrief me later."

The two staffers walked out of the room after exchanging final handshakes.

"So, gentlemen, what can I do for you?"

"To be completely honest, sir, we're just concerned. Lots of buzz going around the Pentagon about what happened to the President. Didn't know if there were any further developments you can share?" Scott asked.

"Well you know I'm not at liberty to expand too much on things, but I feel pretty good that we've got our guy. When all the evidence comes out, I think that will be shown."

"If you need any increased security or anything let us know. Lots of guys at the Pentagon know people in the private sector if you feel you need additional assistance. We're here to help."

"That's great to know. I will definitely let you know if our needs change. Lieutenant Mixson, have we met before? You look so familiar."

"I don't believe we have, sir."

"Okay, men. I have a meeting with the President in five minutes, so I need to run."

"Thank you for your time."

The Vice President walked out, and they headed the other direction.

"Do you think he knew who you were?" Scott asked.

"No, but he might have seen me before and not realized where."

"If he looks up the real Lieutenant Mixson, he'll know it's not you. Then he'll come after us."

"Hey, this was your idea."

"I know. I'm glad we got to talk to him face to face."

"You SEALs will never learn. We did more than talk. I lifted his phone."

"You're kidding?" Scott asked.

"No, I'm not. Let's get out of here." Marc didn't want to waste any time. They needed to look at that phone right away.

CHAPTER TWELVE

iv paced around her living room waiting for Marc to show up. She knew it was probably going to hurt to seeing him in her home after he'd broken her trust in so many ways, but she'd been too weak to refuse him. After tonight, though, she promised herself that she would be done with him for good. She had to be.

When the doorbell rang, she opened the door and saw Marc standing there with daisies in his hands. He'd chosen her favorite flowers. He must have noticed the small daisy accents in her bathroom. She couldn't figure this man out. She wanted to say something but felt tears well up in her eyes. He handed her the flowers, and she took them and walked into the kitchen. She filled a vase with water and put in the flowers. Turning around she expected to see Marc, but he was sitting on the sofa in the living room.

She took a deep breath, walked toward him, and took a seat beside him. She wanted to be close to look him in the eyes and hear his explanation. "All right. Start talking."

"There's some stuff about me I want you to know. But first, I need to give you an update on what Scott and I have found."

She nodded.

"We have uncovered some evidence that may implicate the Vice President."

"What?"

"I know it seems crazy, but there are calls that can't be explained on his phone. And one highly troubling call to Oscar Penzer. How could there be an innocent explanation for him contacting your stalker?"

"How in the world did you get access to his phone?"

"You don't want to know."

"Oh, God." Her mind raced. The Vice President tried to take out the President? Why? "Why would Brett Meyer do this? He's the VP."

"We don't think he was trying to have her killed. At least not yet, anyway. Our theory is that he just wanted her injured to help ensure her re-election. We don't really know what his endgame is."

A cold shiver shot down her arms. "That is awful." She paused and took a deep breath. "How strong is this evidence?"

"It's not highly compelling, but it's enough to raise suspicion. Given how the rest of the events have played out, I think there's something there and so does Scott."

"So he frames us. Then what, he takes out the President once they get re-elected?"

"That's our best theory at this point."

"I don't know what to say. When I said I thought it could be an inside job, I meant Secret Service. Not the freaking Vice President of the United States."

"Like I said, it's not definitive, but it's enough to bother me. You need to watch your back..." Marc paused and then continued, "seeing as I'm not staying with you now."

"I—I'll be careful."

"And now for the reason why I originally wanted to talk to you." He ran a hand through his hair and then looked at her, his dark eyes pleading for something that she couldn't decipher. This man had more secrets than she did.

"I didn't retire from Delta because of the stress on my body."

"All right." Where was he going with this?

"I made a decision in the field in Afghanistan. One that everyone else disagreed with. I felt that my lead was solid. So I pulled rank and my team and I stormed a village outside Kandahar. The intel that I brokered was bad, the key terror suspect we were seeking wasn't there, but the enemy insurgents were. It was a trap."

This sounded awful. She looked over at him and his hands shook just slightly. "What happened?"

"One of my guys was killed. A few injured."

"I'm so sorry."

"I haven't gotten to the worst part."

"Okay." She took a deep breath and waited.

"The guy who was killed was my best friend's brother." Tears sparkled in his eyes.

Her chest tightened and her pulse quickened. "Oh no."

"My best friend was also part of my Delta team and the operation. He strongly fought me on going into the village, but I didn't listen. I was so confident in the intelligence that I brokered that I marched forward with my own plans. And in the end, his brother was killed. I not only lost his brother that day, and caused some of my men to be injured, but I also lost my best friend. He hasn't spoken to me since the day he told me I couldn't attend his brother's funeral."

"Why are you telling me this now?"

"Because I wanted you to know who I really am." He looked down. "One of the worst parts is that my buddy's brother wasn't even an operator on our team. He was just there for a couple of days getting additional training. We were a man down, and so he stepped in. It was the worst possible combination of events."

She broke down and moved right beside him on the couch. Grabbing his hand, she squeezed. She didn't want him to feel like he was alone and hurting any longer. But he hurt her, and she didn't know how all of this added up. "How did you end up at the FBI and on this investigation?"

"I knew I couldn't stay with Delta after what had happened. I'd lost the respect of my team. Granted, there were a lot of people outside my unit who agreed with my call, but in the end it didn't matter. I couldn't stay in."

"I understand."

"I appreciate you saying that, but I don't know if you do. The military was everything to me. It was my entire life. My best friend and I, his name is Shane. We went through Ranger school together. Then we both were selected to join Delta at the same time. He was more than a friend. We call each other brothers in the teams, but Shane truly felt like a brother to me. To see him look at me with such hatred. It almost killed me. I didn't know if I even wanted to live."

"What got you through?"

"The thought that I didn't want Shane's brother to have died in vain. I knew I had to get out, but I thought maybe one day after I regrouped I could avenge his death."

"Wow."

"After a lot of thought, that no longer seemed like the best idea. Revenge wasn't the solution. I needed to do something with my life—to try to make an impact in a different way. So that's when I looked at the FBI. And political corruption. It seemed so very different than the work I'd done before, but in a way similar. Maybe I thought I could find redemption or peace. Even the smallest amount would be a relief."

"And have you?"

"Honestly, no. The pain is still there. I rethink my decision, and my mistake, every single day. And now I've hurt you in a way that I never wanted to." He paused and tightened his grip on her hand. "I really care about you, Viv. I know that I lied to you, and that you have every right to reject me. I want you to know that what I feel for you is real. More real than anything I've felt in a long time. All I'm asking is for you to give me a chance—the real me. With all of my baggage and issues."

She didn't know what to say or how to respond. "Marc I just don't know what to say."

"Do you care about me?"

She knew she couldn't lie. "Yes."

His eyes still glistening, he leaned close to her and pressed his lips to hers. She knew that kiss. That kiss filled with such hunger and passion. He still wanted her, and she still wanted him. But he had deceived her. Could she put it behind her and start over? She didn't know if she could, but at that moment she desperately wanted to try.

"God, I've missed you." He ran his hands through her hair and kissed her neck.

She let herself get lost in the moment. The raw emotion was pouring out of him. She finally felt like she'd seen the real Marc. And this Marc—the real Marc—wanted her. He might think he was damaged, but she had her own issues, even though now wasn't the time to dredge those up. Not when the only thing she wanted was to feel him inside of her. Now.

Feeling her sense of urgency, as she tugged at his clothes, he picked her up from the couch and carried her up the stairs and into the bedroom. While she was expecting hard and fast, he slowed down the pace, exploring every inch of her body with his hands and his tongue. She heard herself making incomprehensible noises.

"Marc, you're killing me."

"Far from it, I'm enjoying you."

She sighed and stopped fighting him, letting him take control and love her. And that's when it hit her. This was the real thing. Love. She'd still have to work out how she'd move past the lies that Marc told her because of the investigation, but at the end of it all she knew that she loved this man. Loved all of him.

"Marc."

"Yeah."

She looked up directly in his eyes. "I love you."

Instead of answering with words, he entered her and she heard herself scream his name. As she felt her body rocked by sensations all she could think about was how she felt about him. Would he feel the same?

Later that night she could hear him breathing and wondered if he was awake like her. She turned to face him and in the dimly lit room could tell his eyes were open.

"You're awake too?" she asked.

"Yeah. I fell asleep, but I've been awake for a bit."

She reached out and ran her hand down his cheek.

"Viv, while we're being open and honest, there's one more thing."

Her heart dropped. What else could there be? "I don't know if I want to hear it."

"I'm going to tell you anyway. This isn't about me. It's about Scott."

"Is he okay?"

"Yeah. It's nothing like that. But he told me something, and I feel like I need to tell you."

"I can only imagine."

"Believe me you won't be expecting this."

"Now you really have me worried."

"Scott didn't cheat on you."

"What? What are you talking about? Of course he did."

He pulled her closer to him. "He just told you that."

"Why in the world would he have made that up?"

"He got cold feet. Thought the relationship was moving too fast. He didn't know a way out. He believed the only way you'd really end things with him is if he used that excuse."

"That is crazy."

"He knows that now, but at the time he felt trapped."

Her heart clenched. Is that the way men felt about relationships? Felt about her? That she trapped them?

"And how do you feel? Do you feel trapped?"

"No," he answered with no hesitation. "I want to be with you, Viv. That's why I'm telling you this now. No more secrets. Even though it wasn't mine to tell, since he told me last night I felt I needed to tell you."

"That is so messed up. I mean, I realized after the fact that we would've never worked. We're better off as friends, but to make up a story like that? Having someone cheat on you is the worst feeling. I felt like I wasn't enough. That I was somehow lacking. Why couldn't he just tell me the truth?"

He ran his hand gently up and down her back. "He's an idiot, and I'm an idiot too. All men are idiots. Right now the only thing that matters, Viv, is that I really care about you. Scott's the past. The distant past."

Her mind was filled with so many thoughts and questions. On one hand, she couldn't believe Scott would've done that, but after hearing it all, it sounded like he had. "Wow. And I thought Scott and I had moved on from everything and had a solid friendship. A true friendship."

He reached over and pulled her into a tight hug, his strong arms enveloping her and providing assurance. "I know you're hurt, but he does value your friendship and wants to make things right."

"I'm sorry, I just had no idea. I feel so dumb. I must seem pretty gullible at the moment."

"No, Viv, you don't. Why would Scott lie about something like that? It's not sane or rational, and you had no way of knowing what I was up to. It was my job to make sure you didn't. And I like to think that, even with all of my failings, I'm good at my current job."

"We don't have to go back over all of that again right now."

"Why don't you try to go back to sleep?" He rubbed his hand gently down her arm.

"You're not the only one with demons, you know?"

She felt his grip tighten in a way that made her feel comforted. "Anything you want to talk about now?"

Might as well put it all out there since Marc had already shared his past with her. "After my parents died. I had nightmares for years. Debilitating nightmares. They're under control now, but it took a while. I had to go to counseling. As you know they died in a car wreck, but they didn't die on impact. They died because their car went up in flames. All that fire. I just couldn't get it out of my mind. Such a horrific way to go, you know?"

"I'm so sorry," he whispered in her ear. He kissed the top of her head and stroked her hair.

"Once they were gone, I was all alone. Starting out at Georgetown, it was supposed to be the happiest time of my life. Instead, I was faced with so many day to day worries. I poured all my energy into school and didn't let a lot of people in. I became a loner. I was the only person I could trust myself not to lose. I was all I had."

She felt the hot tears stream down her cheek. "You have to understand how my experiences with men later in life have not been what I would've wanted them to be. I don't let people into my life all that often, and to find out that Scott lied about cheating on me. That really hurts. To find out that you lied even if it was your job. It just makes me question myself. I always thought I was a pretty good judge of character. Now I'm wondering if I was really wrong."

"Don't say that. Look at who trusts you. Senator Nelson values your opinion and has promoted you to your current position. Also you were right about Arthur, he might be an ass but he's not guilty of murder. And at the end of the day you are a strong, independent, and brilliant woman. Look at what you've accomplished, and you did that on your own. You. And you know what else you've done? You've made me want to do better. To be a better man."

She wiped the tears away and turned so that he was holding her fully. She didn't want to think about her parents, or Scott, or the other hardships she'd faced. For the rest of the night, she only wanted to think about him and all the things he did to make her happy. "Are you tired?" she asked.

"If you're asking because you had something in mind besides sleep, then hell no, I'm not tired."

"Good." She smiled and pressed herself against him.

***

Viv hated to see Marc go the next morning, but he had some work related things he said he had to take care of. Viv knew it most likely had to do with his and Scott's ongoing investigation into the Vice President. Viv still didn't want to believe that the Vice President was behind any of this and was holding out hope that someone else was to blame. She knew Arthur wasn't the culprit though. Even though he was still in custody, he'd expanded his legal team, and she felt it was only a matter of days before he would be released. There was simply not enough evidence to hold him.

Viv opened up her laptop and started doing some additional background research on Vice President Brett Meyer. She had done a lot of opposition research on the President and some on the Vice President, but not nearly as much. She took a sip of coffee and Willow jumped in her lap, making it somewhat difficult to type. She loved when Willow was openly affectionate, so she didn't put her down. Willow purred contentedly as Viv surfed the net, balancing cat, keyboard, and coffee mug.

The notable thing about Brett was that he was a little younger than the President and a favorite of some in his party but not all. He was definitely more ideological than the President. Could he really be the mastermind behind this plot? She shuddered just thinking about it.

A loud knock on the door had Willow flying off her lap. Who could that be on a Saturday morning? She walked over the door and was relieved to see Ralph on the other side through the peephole. She didn't know what he wanted, but at least she felt comfortable with him. She opened the door and smiled.

"Ralph, what are you doing here?"

"Can I come in?"

"Sure."

He walked through the door and stood in the foyer.

"Is something wrong?" she asked.

"Possibly. I need to talk to you about Marc."

"Is he okay?" A million thoughts ran through her head. Could he have been hurt or injured?

"It's not like that. We've been working some angles and have reason to believe that Marc may be behind the attack on the President."

"No," she stuttered. "No. That's not possible."

"Listen to me, Viv. I know you have a thing for the guy, but there's a lot you don't know about him."

She didn't want to hear any of this. There was no way he would've tried to kill the President. And after last night, she didn't doubt his true character. He might not have been honest with her about his reasons for joining the Nelson campaign, but she was certain he wasn't capable of double crossing her again.

"Why don't we have a seat?"

"I'd rather stand."

"I know you're skeptical, but the man you think you know really has issues."

"Like what?"

"He has a vendetta against the President. He holds her responsible for the death of one of his Delta teammates."

"How so?"

"The President was personally involved in an operation that went to hell in a handbasket. Marc didn't want to complete the mission and expressed his concerns, but the President ordered him to proceed. He followed her orders. As a result, a few of his unit were injured and one was killed."

A chill shot down her arm as she realized that she was hearing a very different version of the same story she'd heard last night. Was Marc lying? But why would he have lied? And if he wasn't lying, that meant Ralph was. Her mind frantically evaluated the two accounts: who should she trust? She wasn't altogether sure of herself or her decision, but ultimately she knew that she had to stay composed. Taking a deep breath, she looked down and then back up at Ralph.

"Even if that's true, that doesn't mean he wants to kill the President."

"We've found evidence implicating him. I can't go into details, but you are in danger."

"Danger from Marc?"

"Yes." Ralph's blue eyes were focused on her.

"I don't think Marc would hurt me."

"I know you don't want to believe it, but I have orders to get you out of here. To take you to a safe location."

"Orders from who?" She knew now he was lying. If Marc wanted to hurt her, he could have easily silenced her while she was lying in his arms last night. She was now trapped with Ralph in her condo.

"The Senator. He's worried for your safety."

"Where will you take me?"

"A safe house for now."

Viv quickly weighed her options. She needed a way out. She made the split second decision and would have to live with it.

"All right. Are we leaving now? Do I need to pack a bag and make arrangements for Willow?"

"There's no time. We'll send over another agent for your stuff and take care of your cat."

She nodded. His comments only confirmed her suspicions. She'd have to get ready to make her move. She'd probably only have one shot.

They walked out the door and down the winding sidewalk. His car was parked in front of her condo. Once she got in that car, it was all over. She took a deep breath and knew what she had to do.

Run. She bolted as fast as she could down the street. Ralph was a big athletic guy, but she was fast and ran regularly. Although, if he shot her, it wouldn't matter. She was hoping it wouldn't come to that. Also, if he'd wanted her dead, he could've already killed her.

She heard him curse behind her. He was gaining, but she kept pushing. Her heart pounded, and a fresh trickle of sweat dripped down her back.

"Viv, stop!" he yelled.

But she couldn't stop. Wouldn't stop. Of course, the day when she needed someone to be out in the street, there wasn't a soul in sight. The road went up on a small incline, and she was pushing herself up the hill. She refused to turn around, but she could tell he was gaining. Ralph was in great shape, but so was she. She wasn't going to give up without a fight. She kept running a few blocks until her legs felt like they were going to explode. The burn went through her entire body. Then just like that she knew he had caught up to her. She braced herself as the impact of his huge body tackled her to the hard sidewalk, skinning her knees.

"I didn't want to have to hurt you, Viv." He grabbed her up off the ground.

"Why are you doing this?"

"It's complicated. The less you know the better."

He might not want to kill her now, but before this was all over, she was almost certain she'd be dead.

"We're going to walk back to my car. Don't try anything else. I'm trying to make this easy on you, Viv, I like you. But don't push me. I have a gun, and I will use it."

"I don't understand." She hoped the dumber she played the more information she could get out of him.

"Your boyfriend and his sidekick have been snooping around in places they shouldn't be. They should've let Arthur take the heat. Then everything would've been fine."

"How could you do this, Ralph? You took an oath to protect the President of the United States."

"Nothing is ever as clear cut as it seems, Viv. Nothing."

His last words sounded somewhat resigned. Unable to comprehend what his tone might mean, she stayed quiet. They walked in silence back to his car, his grip tight on her arm. Her stomach churned, and she wondered what was next. They could never let her live given what she knew. The fact that they hadn't killed her outright meant they were planning on using her for something in the interim. She felt sick thinking about what would happen to Marc and Scott. And she was helpless, having no way to warn them.

"Who is behind this, Ralph?"

He didn't respond. She knew it wasn't him. He was just following orders. The question was, who was giving them—the Vice President? Or someone else?

He opened the door to the back seat, and she saw him reach for something from the front seat. The last thing she heard him say as he turned to her was: "I'm sorry, Viv."

Before she could do anything, he put something over her mouth. She took a deep breath to scream, and her world went black.

CHAPTER THIRTEEN

Marc knew something was terribly wrong. Viv wasn't at her condo, but all of her stuff was there, including her purse, cell phone, and laptop. Her front door was also unlocked. He'd planned on letting himself in, but hadn't needed to use the key he still had.

Damn, he should've never left her. Just one more in a series of bad moves on his part. But now wasn't the time to feel sorry for himself. He had to find her. He dialed Scott who he had just left an hour ago.

"Ranger," he said.

"We've got a big problem. Viv's gone. Has she contacted you?"

"No, I haven't heard anything. What do you mean she's gone?"

"I got back to the condo, and she's not here. But all of her stuff is."

"Shit."

"We've got to find her and fast. This doesn't feel good. I'm headed up to Nelson campaign headquarters. Can you meet me there?"

"Yeah."

"Scott, watch your six."

"Roger that."

By the time Marc reached campaign headquarters to meet Scott his head was spinning. They stormed through the front door. The office was dead. Given the recent events, staffing had been reduced which was only made worse because it was a weekend.

Marc scanned the room looking for Ralph, thinking perhaps he'd have a lead. Instead he saw another Secret Service agent.

"Where's Ralph?"

"He called in this morning saying that he's taking a few days off."

Marc looked over at Scott. Ralph had to be involved somehow. This was all too coincidental. Marc turned his attention back to the agent. "Do you have any idea where he's at?"

"No. You can try his cell, but I know when I'm on vacation I turn off completely. Let the crew that's working manage the issues."

Marc didn't know who he could trust right now besides Scott. A quick glance in Scott's direction let him know they were on the same page.

"Thanks. We'll see you later." Marc nodded to the agent and walked toward the door with Scott beside him.

"We've got to find Ralph," Scott said quietly.

"I feel like if we find Ralph then we find Viv. Got any ideas?"

"If the circumstances weren't so bad, I'd be bragging right now."

"What did you do?"

"I put a GPS tracker on Ralph's car."

"You suspected him?" Marc asked.

"Well, if I'm being totally honest, I put trackers on all those I possibly suspected. And that means, I basically tagged all the cars I could find whose owners were listed in the Vice President's personal address book and had been contacted within the past month."

"We need to think about how to proceed. I don't know how much under the radar our little investigation still is. I just I hope we won't be too late to find Viv. We're going to need a lot of supplies."

"What do you have at your place?" Scott asked.

"Enough gear and ammo to do some serious damage. You?"

"The same."

"All right. Let's get loaded up and track down that bastard."

* * *

Viv woke up with a pounding headache. She tried to move and realized her hands were tied behind her back to a chair. Her neck ached, and her entire body throbbed. Then it hit her. She remembered what had happened with Ralph. Not only had she hit the pavement when he'd tackled her, but she'd also been drugged and knocked out by something. As she came to, she took a moment to look at her surroundings. The room was small and dimly lit. Besides the chair she was tied to there wasn't any other furniture.

She craned her neck up and looked at the ceiling. It appeared like she was in some sort of warehouse. It was very quiet except for water dripping from some unknown source. She wondered if she'd been left there to die. But that wouldn't make sense. Someone had a plan for her and whatever it was, it had to be bad. Scenarios flew through her head. She was worried about Marc and Scott. But she was also very concerned about the Senator and hoped to God he was safe. Were they planning on hurting him too?

She struggled against the rope, but it was tied too tightly. Her hands were already feeling numb. She needed to conserve some energy. Whatever sedative Ralph had used on her had taken its toll.

She closed her eyes and said a prayer. She hadn't prayed much since the death of her parents, but right now she knew she needed a miracle. She did not want to die like this, not after fighting so hard to get to where she was. Not after overcoming all of her demons. And definitely not after falling in love with Marc. She might be a fool to want a future with him, but right now the thought of not having one was unthinkable.

Unable to stop the tears, she let them flow. There was nothing she could do right now. She hated the helpless feeling deep in her gut. *Think.* She had to think. She was a fighter.

She heard a noise. The sound of footsteps outside the room was getting closer. Light flooded into the room and three shadowy figures emerged. Her heart dropped. There standing in front of her was Ralph, the mystery man, and the Vice President of the United States. Her fears were confirmed. The Vice President was a traitor.

"Ms. Reese. I trust you're comfortable?" The Vice President said with a sinister smile.

"I don't know what you're doing here, Mr. Vice President, but I would strongly urge you to rethink it. It's not too late."

He laughed and looked at Ralph and then the mystery man. "Give us a few minutes alone."

"Are you sure?" Ralph asked. His blue eyes were full of concern.

This was not good. What did the Vice President have on Ralph to make him look at her with worry? And who was this other guy? Whoever he was, he gave Viv the creeps.

"Yes, yes. I'm not going to hurt her."

Somehow she didn't believe that for one second. Brett Meyer might have looked harmless to most people standing there in his designer suit with a calm expression on his face but underneath that exterior, there was a monster. One she was just now seeing.

Ralph and the mystery man slowly walked out of the room. Brett strode over to her and patted her shoulder. She tried not to recoil at his touch, not that she could move much.

"Let me explain what's going to happen here, Ms. Reese. You actually have a few options."

She looked up at him and didn't say a word.

"A lot of how this ends up for you depends on your level of cooperation. I have no personal issue with you. You got stuck in the wrong place at the wrong time. If it wasn't for Gene's unfortunate heart attack, then we wouldn't be having this conversation right now."

"What's your point?" she asked, gaining a little courage.

"Here's how this will play out. You can help me, and in turn I will help you."

"Help you how?"

"By framing your new boyfriend."

She sucked in a breath.

"Oh, I see that doesn't immediately appeal to you. But I think that once you take some time and consider it, you will be more amendable to that option."

"You said I had a few options."

"Yes, but they only get less favorable for you."

"I'm listening." She needed to get as much information from him as she could. If that meant holding her tongue and not telling him he could take his options and go to hell, then she'd have to do it.

"The second option is that you will take the fall. I have everything I need to make an air tight case against you or really whomever I choose."

"No one would believe that I tried to kill the President."

"To the contrary, the people that work for me are very good. I have the best resources in the United States at my disposal. I can assure you that there would be no dispute."

"Any more options?"

"Sure. Option three is you die a tragic death. An accident. A house fire, perhaps. Sadly you didn't wake up in time."

When he said fire, she felt her body convulse. She couldn't go back there right now. He had to have known what happened to her parents. How it affected her and how their painful deaths haunted her for years. But she couldn't let him win. Just as she hadn't let her nightmares win.

"Are you trying to play mind games now, Mr. Vice President? You didn't strike me as the type." She looked straight into his liquid blue eyes.

He laughed. "You know, I actually like you, Ms. Reese. I sincerely hope you'll choose option number one. But in the end, the choice is yours. I'm a gentleman in that way. I'll let you in on a little secret. Mind games are my favorite kind. They were how I got into politics. It's my ability to play them and win that brought me to the White House and will help keep me there."

She had to struggle not to spit in his face. This man could not be allowed to become President.

"You may think you're in love with that Delta punk, but you're not. You're too good for him. What kind of man lets his own men get slaughtered? He's a failure."

She looked him in the eyes, desperately wanting to defend Marc. But now wasn't the time.

"I'll let you think this over."

"Why do I have to stay tied up?"

"I'm not stupid, Ms. Reese. Ralph told me you gave him quite a run. I don't want to encourage you. But just in case, let me assure you that we are in a secure location. Even if you were to get out of this room, you wouldn't get very far. However, if you agree to cooperate, then I will ensure you will be more comfortable."

She eyed him warily and nodded. There wasn't much else she could do.

"One more thing. Your Navy SEAL friend has really become a thorn in my side. He paid a visit to my office the other day, and I have the sinking suspicion that he took my phone."

"I don't know what you're talking about."

"Fine. But know that he's a loose end. However, I might be able to keep him around for a little bit longer if he agrees to help me."

Obviously this guy had no idea who he was dealing with. Scott would sooner die than help a traitor. The Vice President walked out, and she was left alone with her thoughts. He would not let her live. Yeah, he wanted her help in framing Marc. But since she knew the truth, she too was a loose end. He would never let her just go on living her life. Not that she would want to if Marc was dead. She shuddered, thinking about the fact that this man could be the next President of the United States. She couldn't let that happen.

* * *

Marc took a deep breath after he ended the tense call with Peter. He and Scott had made the strategic decision not to tell anyone about the operation until they were close to the location. Then he'd convinced Peter to bring in only a core FBI group. He'd gotten the go ahead to proceed first. Another team would be in route soon. But that didn't help in the here and now. It had been a long afternoon getting ready for this mission which included doing more intelligence gathering on Ralph and getting all of their supplies in order. Now it was nightfall. Marc may have seemed calm on the outside, but on the inside his gut was churning.

Scott was behind the wheel and they were tracking down Ralph. According to the GPS, they were getting close. It didn't surprise him that they were winding their way through an industrial district in Virginia not too far from DC. His pulse raced, and he was angry, not to mention worried about Viv. If he saw Ralph right now, it would be hard not to snap his neck. He'd trusted Ralph. What a mistake. He couldn't help but beat himself up. Images of Viv hurt, injured, and the worst possibility—the image of finding her lifeless body kept flashing through his head.

He turned his attention back to the GPS. "We're closing in. Almost there."

"This is going to get ugly. The only question is how fast."

"We should stop here and proceed on foot. Darkness is our friend."

"Roger that." Scott pulled over to the side of the road and parked behind one of the industrial warehouses. "According to GPS, Ralph's car is about a mile away. It's not moving."

Virginia was about the furthest place in the world from the mountains of Afghanistan, but he had a momentary flashback as he stepped out of Scott's car. It was just the two of them against an unknown number of forces. Neither of them had any clue what they were really up against, but he felt it would be a lot more than just one rouge Secret Service agent. They had agreed not to go in guns blazing. The goal wasn't to attack and take out enemy forces—but to rescue Viv. If they had the opportunity to capture those who needed to be brought to justice that was just icing on the cake. But in the end, they'd do whatever was necessary to accomplish the mission.

Each man was wired with recording equipment. Given the stakes they needed this to be documented. Peter had insisted on it. As they both put on their night vision goggles, their tactical gear was complete.

"Your shoulder going to be okay?" Marc asked.

"Yeah. My rehab is over halfway done."

"Let's move," Marc said.

Scott didn't respond but started walking. They'd been trained for this and moved towards the location of the GPS signal at a light jog. They darted in between the warehouses, staying low when they didn't have sufficient cover. As far as Marc could tell, there wasn't a soul in sight, but that didn't mean anything.

Scott pulled out the GPS and made a hand signal. This was it. He saw the car parked behind a large warehouse. Ralph had to be in there. And hopefully Viv was too. The night air was warm and sweat beaded on his forehead.

It was go time. "Let's scout around the building. Then we can decide where we enter," Marc whispered.

"I'm thinking the best option is through the roof. Those ventilation shafts." Scott pointed.

Marc nodded, and they began their trek around the building. It would be difficult without having the building's schematics, but they didn't have the time or the resources at their disposal. Marc noted one main entrance, with a garage type door in the rear. Scott was probably right. Going in through the roof was most likely the best option. Clearly they weren't going to walk in through the front door. He hoped they'd have the element of surprise on their side, but he wouldn't assume anything right now.

"It's our lucky day. There's some partial scaffolding on the side over there. Let's move it over and use it. I'd put on your gloves, so you don't get cut on any stray metal shards."

"You ready to climb?" Marc asked. He knew Scott would be. Scaling the building wouldn't be an issue for either man.

"I'll go first," Scott said. "If the insulation isn't good, they'll hear us coming. I'll try to tread as lightly as possible. Just be aware. Things could heat up quickly."

Marc watched through his night vision goggles as Scott easily made his way up the warehouse on the unsteady scaffolding even with a bum shoulder. Deep in his gut he still couldn't believe this was all happening. Yeah, he knew politicians were corrupt. But the Vice President was more than corrupt. He was a traitor. His treasonous acts against the United States and the President made Marc ill. He thought of all his buddies who had died or been gravely injured serving this country. There was no way he'd let Brett Meyer get away with this. He absolutely could not be the man controlling his brothers in arms. He knew that Scott felt the same way. The unspoken understanding between them was clear. Once Viv was rescued, they'd do whatever it took to make sure he was stopped.

It was Marc's turn and the scaffolding wobbled under his weight. He was relieved to find jutted out metal grooves on the warehouse to help maintain his balance. He was on the rooftop quickly. Scott was crouched down low, looking at the ventilation grates.

"What have we got?" Marc asked.

"They're rusty as hell, but we should be able to get them off. Just as a heads up it will be a tight squeeze, hope you've kept up your workout routine."

Both men went to work prying the ventilation cover off.

"Don't move," a deep voice said. For a split second, Marc considered taking a chance and going for his gun. He was an impeccable shot. He might even get the jump on the guy, but it was too big of a risk.

"We could hear your footsteps the moment you climbed up. Not exactly a covert op."

It was Ralph. He did have a gun on them, but this was two against one. Marc looked over at Scott. Scott made a little hand signal. They weren't going to be doing anything yet. They needed to get inside that warehouse. Ralph was now their ticket in.

"C'mon, you two. Don't even think about trying anything. Drop you guns on the ground now. Slowly."

Marc and Scott didn't have a choice and did as Ralph instructed.

"There are two more men on the ground waiting for you. Don't make any stupid moves."

Ah. Brett had a little cadre of traitors working for him.

"Where's Viv?" Marc asked.

"She's fine for now. That's all you need to know."

"Why, Ralph?"

"It's complicated. We don't have time for chit chat right now. I've got a special friend who would like to talk to you, Marc."

Marc had no choice but to scale down the side of the warehouse where two men were waiting with guns drawn.

Ralph was right behind him. "Locke, you're with me. You two, take the SEAL with you. Keep him quiet."

So they were separating them. He had to hand it to Ralph, so far he was making all the right moves. However, Marc knew that Scott could take care of himself. Ralph seemed to have something brewing, but he wasn't sure what.

"Let's go. Stay close," Ralph said, as he grabbed his arm.

"You sure you don't want to talk about this Ralph? You're a smart guy. We can figure a way out of this for you. It's not too late."

"This isn't up for negotiation," he barked. "Keep moving."

Ralph led him through the front door of the warehouse. He surveyed his surroundings. The building looked deserted with a few crates and boxes but not much of anything else. He could see a couple of doors leading to other rooms. He wondered if Viv was behind one of them.

"In here," Ralph said, as he pushed Marc to one of the doors.

Ralph opened the door and shoved Marc in. Standing in the corner with a snide smile was the Vice President.

"Nice to meet again, Mr. Locke. Or no, it's Lieutenant Gary Mixson?" Brett laughed. "Did you really think you could waltz into my office in the White House and pull that shit with me?"

"I'm having a hard time understanding what is going on here, sir. Why don't you explain it to me?" He felt his fists clench. Ralph stood to his side, with his gun drawn.

"It's quite simple. We've detected a threat against our great President. That threat is Ms. Vivian Reese. She's here right now. That's why the Secret Service is here with me. There's evidence implicating her in the attempt on the President's life." Brett took a deep breath and continued. "You're a good soldier, Marc. I could use another man like you on my team. Once I'm President, you can have your pick of posts."

"And what do you want from me in return?"

"Your testimony against Viv."

Marc held back his visceral reaction of disgust and contempt. He knew Viv wasn't involved in the assassination attempt, but he didn't want to give to this man any clues to the cards he was holding. "Why would I do that?"

"Because at the end of the day, she's just another woman to you. It's not like you're one to be tied down by relationships of any kind. And this way, you'd be able to restore your good name after that unfortunate incident in Afghanistan. It's a win-win for you, my friend."

"And the President?"

"Leave her up to me."

"Where's Viv?"

"She's here. But right now I need to know your answer to my proposal."

"I want to know that she's safe before I talk to you anymore."

"You aren't in a position to make demands."

He had limited options. Basically no options. His best was to pretend to go along with it and see if he could rescue Viv in the process. "When you say any post I want, are there any limits?"

Brett laughed. "I get veto power of course. But assuming that what you ask for is in my power to grant, I'd be happy to reward loyal service. You can even head up my security detail if you would like."

He hoped that Viv was still alive and unharmed. He had his doubts, but had to hold onto the belief that she'd be okay. Brett was so calm—discussing treason and murder like it was shooting the shit about a football game. It occurred to Marc that Brett might be crazy. Why was Ralph involved in this mess?

"I accept your deal."

"I knew it." Brett walked over and extended his hand. It took all of his willpower not to grab him, flip him over, and snap his neck.

"Ralph, I told you I could bargain with this guy. I'm glad you brought him to me."

Ralph nodded, but his expression was unreadable.

Before Marc could formulate his next move, the door flew open. Scott burst in with his gun drawn. Without hesitation, Scott shot Ralph in the leg, and he hit the ground hard with a yelp. Brett was already running out the other door to the adjoining room. The man Marc recognized from the campaign shooting video charged into the room. Marc dove toward him, and a shot went off. Damn, that was close. Scott tossed him a gun, and he took a shot at another one of Brett's men who rushed in. It was a kill shot. There was no time for games now. He had no idea how many more men there were. He reached down in his boot and grabbed his knife.

"Enough," a loud voice rang out. "One more shot and she's dead." Brett stood behind Viv, towering over her. A gun to her temple.

He saw the pleading look in Viv's crystal blue eyes. "Mr. Vice President. Just put down the gun. We can sort this out."

Brett grinned. "I'm not as stupid as those helping me. That's one of the reasons I wanted your assistance even if it was only temporary. But that deal is off the table seeing as you've already betrayed our bargain. Things are going to have to go differently now."

Marc knew what he had to do. Brett was erratic. Marc felt the knife in his hand—gripped tightly. He hoped that Scott was paying attention to what was going on. Saying a small prayer, he needed this to be the right move. He couldn't miss. If he did, he might as well just die right now. He couldn't handle another wrong judgment call, and he surely couldn't handle something happening to Viv. But if he didn't act now, Brett was probably going to kill her.

With one flick of his wrist, Marc threw the knife. It hit Brett right on target in the throat. Brett's arm dropped away from Viv's temple, and a shot rang out as he went down.

Then suddenly, Marc felt the pressure of a bullet as it entered his side and tore through his flesh.

* * *

Viv's world was moving in slow motion. She hit the ground hard and saw the blood flowing from Marc's side. She heard herself screaming. Looking down she saw the Vice President lying in a pool of blood moaning. He was still alive. Scott crouched down by Marc, in the process of trying to stop the bleeding.

"Viv," Scott yelled. "Take this gun. Shoot anyone that comes in here. And I mean anyone."

Viv felt numb as she took the gun from Scott. She was also bleeding from where Brett had quickly cut the rope from her wrists.

"Help me," Brett whispered.

She looked down and saw him. And as much as she hated him and what he stood for, she was better than him. She squatted down beside him and used the bloody knife now lying on the ground to cut off a piece of his fancy suit jacket. She tried to apply pressure to his collarbone. He was bleeding a lot, but it didn't look like Marc had hit a major artery.

"Why?" she asked him.

"Because I should've been the President. Never her. I should've been the most powerful man in the world."

"You could've just waited. You're young enough."

"No," he gasped. "It was my time. This race. This was it."

He closed his eyes, but she checked and his pulse was still strong. She didn't think he would die, but he was now unconscious. She ran over to Marc.

"How's he doing?" she asked Scott.

"Lots of blood loss, and he's passed out. Our backup is only minutes out. Hopefully the ambulance will be here soon."

She watched Scott re-apply pressure to Marc's wound as he stripped him of some of his tactical vest, and she felt tears stream down her face. "Do you think he's going to make it?"

Scott reached out and gave her a quick hug. "Yeah. He's a tough SOB. This ain't gonna get him."

She grabbed Marc's hand and leaned down to his ear. "Don't die on me, Marcus Locke. I love you."

* * *

Viv had been at the hospital too much lately. First with Gene and now with Marc. She hated hospitals. She sat in the waiting room with Scott. Over the past few hours before they had arrived at the hospital, Scott was able to debrief the Secret Service and the Pentagon. He'd handed over all his research, including the VP's personal phone log, along with the recording devices that both he and Marc had been wearing throughout the mission. The good news was that Marc had made it through surgery and was now stable. They were waiting to go in and see him when he woke up. But Viv wouldn't feel okay until she touched him and saw him herself. She shivered and wrapped the blanket around her that one of the nurses had given her.

"Want more coffee?" Scott asked.

"No. I think if I drink anymore I'm going to have to start running laps around the floor."

Scott smiled. "You know, I don't know if this is the best time, but since we're both here there is something I want to talk to you about."

She looked over into his big green eyes. "If it concerns the way we broke up, Marc already told me."

"He did?" he asked with a raised eyebrow.

"Yeah. I was pretty upset with you when I first found out. But honestly, so much has happened over the past couple of days. I feel like it's stupid to be upset now."

"Please let me apologize and try to explain."

She nodded.

"I was a world class idiot. I totally flipped out. I got inside my head, and started thinking about you wanting to get married and have a family. And I just wasn't ready. Not even close. I'm not sure I'll ever be ready, Viv. I didn't want to hurt you, but then in the end I lied to you and hurt you in the worst way."

"I'm not going to lie to you, Scott. The thought of you cheating on me was unbearable. I never thought you would stray. I believed that you were too honorable and honest. That's why it was so shocking to hear you admit to cheating."

"And I wouldn't have."

"What were you thinking? What in the world made you think it was a good idea to concoct such a story?"

"I was a coward. I didn't have the nerve to break it off with you. Things were going so well and I thought I wouldn't have the strength to really stay way. I wanted things to remain exactly the way they were, but I thought you wanted things to progress forward. I knew if I said I cheated on you that would be the ultimate deal breaker."

"You were right about that."

"The only reason I bring this up now is I don't want you to think of Marc in the same way. He was doing what he had to do—he was under orders from the FBI. It wasn't his choice to deceive you, and I don't think he meant for a relationship to develop. But you're amazing, and I understand why he couldn't help falling for you."

She smiled. "You really like him, don't you?"

"Yeah, I do. I think we both were ready to pounce when we first met, but once I got to know him, he's a good guy. He's had a hard time out there. War is not pretty, Viv. I know you know that. But he has a good heart, and he's really crazy about you."

The tears started welling up in her eyes. "I'm crazy about him too. I can't lose him."

"Ah, it's okay. Come here." He put his arm around her, and she leaned her head on his shoulder. "He's going to be fine. The fact that he made it through surgery is huge. He'll be his old self in no time."

"Thanks, Scott. For what it's worth, while I don't think what you did to me was right, I am relieved that I was right about your true character. You're still someone I trust even if I want to smack you for what you did to me."

"Fair enough."

"Viv!"

Viv looked up and saw her best friend running toward her. "Rena." She hugged her tight.

"I'm so sorry I couldn't get here faster. As you can imagine, things are an absolute zoo at the White House. I can't even get into it, but it's a mess."

Rena looked over at Scott and frowned. "Hello, Scott."

"Hey, Rena."

She turned her attention back to Viv. "How's Marc?"

"Stable, thank God. We're waiting on him to wake up. The surgery went well."

Tears started flowing down Serena's face.

"What's wrong?" Viv asked.

"Remember the man I told you about?"

"The Secret Service agent?" Viv asked. Her stomach dropped as she suddenly had an idea what was wrong.

"Yeah. Turns out he was involved with the Vice President." Serena started crying harder, and Viv pulled her in tight.

"I am so sorry, Rena."

"How could I have been so wrong? He wasn't cheating on me. It was even worse. He committed treason. I've dedicated my life to working to better this country. I'm beyond sick about this."

Scott walked over to them and put his hand on Serena's shoulder. "Rena, I know I'm not your favorite person. Viv can fill you in later on all the details of things we've worked through. But I'm here for you if you need me." He handed her some tissues, and she nodded.

Viv's heart broke for her friend. Serena was already in an awful situation given the scandal. Now this only made matters worse.

"Hello," a female voice said.

Viv turned and saw the doctor.

"Mr. Locke is awake. All signs are looking favorable. You can go see him, but don't tire him out. He's going to need his rest."

"Thank you, doctor."

"You've got yourself a tough one, there." The doctor smiled, and Viv's heart swelled.

***

Marc felt like crap. His side ached, and his mouth hadn't been this dry since his first tour in Afghanistan when his team got trapped without supplies for days. He knew he was in a hospital. He'd been shot. What he didn't know was what had happened to everyone else. He'd tried to ask the nurse, but she wasn't saying anything.

The door opened, and his heart almost stopped when he saw Viv walk through with Scott right behind her. They were alive. He let out a deep breath and felt the pain shoot through his ribs.

Viv walked over to his bedside and grabbed his hand. "I'm so glad to see you," she said.

"Me too. Are you all right?"

"Yes, I'm fine. Just minor stuff. How are you feeling?"

"Like I've been shot."

She smiled and gripped his hand tighter.

"Nice to see you haven't lost your edge," Scott said.

"How did you manage to get out of there in one piece?"

"You did all the hard work," Scott said.

"What happened to the Vice President?"

"He lost a lot of blood, but he's stable now. He's going to be charged with a variety of crimes including treason and several accounts of attempted murder. As you can imagine this has taken over the news cycle twenty four seven. May be the biggest story in U.S. history."

"Were you two interviewed?"

"Yeah," Viv said. "About fifty times. Same thing over and over. I think they had to make sure that our stories checked out. It also helped that Ralph flipped immediately."

"Why was he involved?"

"Brett was blackmailing him. He has a child with his high school sweetheart. They aren't together anymore, but he still has a big role in his daughter's life. Brett threatened to kill his kid if he didn't cooperate."

This was even uglier than he'd thought. "Is the child safe now?"

"Yes. Everyone is accounted for."

"And the other Secret Service agents?"

"There were a few others. Plus some hired thugs—including the mystery man. They're all in custody. And one of them admitted to doctoring the video to try to frame Viv for the vandalism."

"Can I talk to Viv for a minute?" Marc asked.

Scott nodded and walked out of the room leaving him alone with Viv.

"I need to say this, Viv."

"All right."

He took a deep breath and looked into her beautiful blue eyes. "I love you, Vivian Reese."

Tears welled up in her eyes. "I love you, too."

"I'm sorry I didn't say it before. You mean too much to me."

"Don't worry about anything. You just need to rest and get your strength back. I'll be here. I'm not going anywhere."

"You promise."

"Yes." She leaned down and kissed him.

He closed his eyes and went to sleep.

***

A month later

"I can't believe it's finally here. Election day," Viv said to herself. Her mind raced with so many different emotions. The polls had been totally erratic. Most people sympathized with the President—after all she was shot and betrayed by her own Vice President. But on the other hand, there was a great distrust around her entire administration. Viv thought that Senator Nelson had a good chance of winning, but she wasn't going to get overzealous.

She walked into campaign headquarters for an early morning meeting with the Senator, Arthur, and Abby. Thankfully, Arthur had been cleared of all wrongdoing. And for that matter the Nelson campaign had been too. Not just for suspicion related to the scandal connected to the VP but also cleared of any illegal campaign finance issues. It turned out that the evidence was planted by the Vice President's team. They wanted options in case their other strategies didn't work out.

"Let's talk about the game plan for today," Arthur said. "Senator, you'll go cast your vote first thing this morning in Virginia. Then you'll make a couple of other appearances around town. The final strategy call last night was made that you won't be flying anywhere today for last minute campaign stops. The Governor will meet you this afternoon here for the final meetings and preparation for this evening. We think the American people are ready to vote."

"I fully support that," the Senator said. "Abby, what are the latest polls saying?"

"They're all over the map, Senator. Given the special circumstances, I just don't know if we can read anything into the polls. Viv is going to be out there today in the media, pushing any last minute messaging."

"That's right. Anything that comes up, just let me know and I'm on it." She looked at the door, and Marc stood there.

"Ah, it looks like my security escort is here. I'm off to make the TV rounds."

The Senator stood up and walked over to Marc. "Thank you, again. For everything." He shook his hand.

"I'm here to serve, Senator. Let me know if you need anything from me today. I'll be with Viv unless otherwise instructed."

"No, no. Stay with her. We've got new Secret Service detail that will go with me. They've been vetted and vetted and then re-vetted. I feel comfortable with the group."

Viv and Marc walked out of headquarters hand in hand.

"This is a big day for you," he said.

She laughed. "No pressure or anything."

"I didn't mean it like that. You're going to do great. I just want you to soak it all in. You deserve it."

"We still have to win, Marc."

"I know, but I have a gut feeling on this one."

"I'm glad you do." She leaned in and kissed him before they got in the car. "Let's do this."

* * *

The room was filled with excitement. The downtown DC hotel ballroom had been transformed into a festive party. The President had just delivered a moving and gracious concession speech that was shown on the big screen. Now everyone anxiously waited for Senator Nelson's victory speech. Viv glanced over at Marc looking so handsome in his dark suit and blue tie. She loved that man so much. Knowing that he loved her filled her heart with joy.

Confetti was already dropping as the final states were called for Senator Nelson. For the last hour though, everyone knew it was a foregone conclusion. Viv had given her input to the speech—a speech largely written by the Senator himself. All the campaign workers and volunteers were jubilant. It had been a crazy ride, and all of the hard work was paying off. This was just what the country needed, especially in the face of such an ugly scandal.

"Take it all in, Viv. This is your night," Marc said as squeezed her hand.

"It's like a dream," she said. "After everything that has happened to now have this ending. It's amazing."

"Hey, you," a voice said from behind her.

She turned around to see Serena and Scott. "Serena." She hugged her friend tightly. "You didn't have to come here."

"Yes, I did. I know what a big night this is for you. I wouldn't have missed it for the world."

"But what about the President?"

"She sent us all home. Said to take the rest of the night off. We'll start planning for the transition tomorrow. She was in remarkably good spirits."

"I think she was ready to go, if you ask me. Being the president is no easy task," Scott said. "Especially given all the crap she went through."

A large roar went through the crowd. "It's time," Viv said. She hurried up toward the front with Marc right behind her. "C'mon," she motioned to the others.

She couldn't control the emotion as she listened to the Senator's words. Tears of joy fell down her cheeks, and Marc wrapped his arm tightly around her shoulder.

The party went on for hours, and Viv didn't want to miss a second of it. Marc was there by her side every step of the way. Finally, it started to wind down.

"You ready to go home?" he asked.

"Only if you're coming with me."

"Viv, I never want to let you go. I know we haven't been together that long, but I want us to start thinking about our future together. For good."

Viv smiled. "Let's go home."

EPILOGUE

Ten months later

"Marc, I've got someone here to see you," Scott said as he poked his head into the groom's suite.

"All right." Marc looked up and his stomach dropped. There in front of him was the last person in the world he would've expected to be there. "Shane," he said. He didn't have any other words.

"I'll leave you two alone for a minute," Scott said as he shut the door.

"What are you doing here?"

"Did you think I'd miss your wedding?" Shane said.

"But, we haven't talked."

"I know, man. I needed time. A lot of time. When Scott contacted me and gave me the rundown on things, I decided I needed to man up. I've been through a lot of therapy. I was so angry. Not just angry at you. Angry at the military. Angry at the world. Angry at myself."

"Shane. I'm so sorry. If I could go back and listen to you, you know I would. I think about my decision every single day."

"I'm working on moving on, and you need to move on, too. I hear you have a beautiful lady you're about to marry. I've seen her on TV. She needs you to be all in. My brother would want us to live our lives. I know he wouldn't blame you. When we signed up, we knew the risks. All of us did. I was just hurting too bad to remember that. It was easier for me to direct my anger at you rather than at things that couldn't be controlled."

Shane walked over and gave him a bear hug. "I'm not going to get all choked up. I just wanted to be here and support you now. Because God knows I didn't support you before."

"You have no idea what that means to me."

Scott knocked on the door and walked back in all smiles. "It's time. Let's get you hitched."

***

"Viv, don't you start crying again," Serena said. "This is your wedding day."

"I know. I'm just so happy." She took the tissue and dabbed her eyes.

"We can't have you looking all red eyed in the pictures."

"Did you check on the guys?" Viv asked.

"Yeah. Marc is ready to roll. Totally calm. Scott is a bit more crazy, running around making sure everyone is where they're supposed to be."

"I still can't believe they've grown so close. It was a rocky start between them. I'm thankful that Marc has a friend like Scott now."

"He is a great friend. Do you know what he did for Marc today?"

"What are you talking about, aside from standing up as his best man?"

"He tracked down Marc's old best friend. The one he had the falling out with. He's here today."

"Oh my God. Do you think that's a good idea?"

"Scott said he had it under control."

Viv pulled out another tissue.

"Don't you start that again. You look gorgeous."

President Nelson had insisted on walking Viv down the aisle. When he took her arm, she paused a moment to grieve for the loss of her father. But she was grateful that the President was in her life.

She looked down toward the alter and saw the man she loved. In his Army dress blue uniform, he looked more amazing than she'd ever seen him. When she stood across from him, he grabbed her hands.

"I love you," he whispered.

"I love you, too."

"Let's say our vows and get the honeymoon started." He smiled and winked.

"That's a great idea."

ABOUT THE AUTHOR

Rachel Kall writes romantic suspense. She likes writing spicy and suspenseful stories to keep readers guessing. She loves animals and is active in animal rescue. She enjoys adding loveable pets to her stories. She lives in Georgia with her husband and five furkids—two dogs and three cats.

Connect online:
Facebook: www.facebook.com/AuthorRachelKall
Twitter: @RachelKall
Website: www.RachelKall.com

ALSO BY RACHEL KALL

Legally Undercover
Edge of Your Seat Romantic Suspense

Attorney Alex Popov's dream of partnership is put to the test when she's pulled into a top-secret investigation involving arms dealers and one of her clients, Rodrigues Capital. The only good part about her association with the secretive organization is her client contact, Pedro Martín. She's drawn to him, but he's hiding something.

When Jacob shows up as a new attorney at Alex's firm, it's clear Pedro isn't the only one with secrets. As Alex tries to determine Jacob's true identity, she's drawn closer to Pedro and deeper into the mystery of Rodrigues Capital and its shadowy networks.

Everyone has an agenda. In a world of lies, where no one is what they seem, Alex puts everything—even her dreams of partnership—on the line for love.

WHAT'S NEXT BY RACHEL KALL

Presidential Pursuit
A Prequel Novella

Dynamic and determined, Helen Riley has devoted her life to public service. Now she's on the verge of doing something no other woman has ever done: Become the President of the United States of America. But her enemies will stop at nothing to end her Presidential hopes.

Smart, loyal, and sexy Sean Mackay has never pushed to be more than Governor Riley's best friend and strongest supporter. However, when her life is threatened Sean steps up to protect the woman he loves beyond all reason.

As the campaign heats up, sparks begin to fly between Helen and Sean. Will she make history and admit her love for Sean, or will her pursuit of the White House end in tragedy?

THANK YOU

Thank you for reading *Race to Kill*. I really hope you enjoyed this story. If you did, please consider helping others enjoy this book too by:

Recommending it! Please help other readers find this book by recommending it to friends, readers' groups, and discussion boards.

Reviewing it! Please tell other readers why you liked this book by reviewing it at Amazon or Goodreads, or any other retail outlet.

Made in the USA
San Bernardino, CA
15 April 2014